FROM THE
NANCY DREW FILES

THE CASE: Time is running short for George—she's been kidnapped to divert Nancy's attention from an ivory smuggling investigation in Alaska.

CONTACT: Carson Drew's old friend, Alaskan shipping magnate Henry Wilcox, is the police department's primary suspect in the smuggling case.

SUSPECTS: Steve Wilcox—Henry's son seems more interested in keeping Nancy away from his upcoming sled-dog race than in helping her clear his father.

John Tilden—Wilcox's butler grows nervous around Nancy . . . especially when the subject of his past employment comes up.

Amanda Spear—a bookkeeper in Wilcox's firm, her salary doesn't come close to paying for the jewelry and the clothes she wears.

COMPLICATIONS: Steve Wilcox would like nothing better than to see more of George—while Steve's ex-girlfriend, Amanda Spear, would like nothing better than to see George disappear.

Books in The Nancy Drew Files™ Series

Available from ARCHWAY Paperbacks

THE
NANCY DREW
FILES™

Case 53
TRAIL OF LIES

CAROLYN KEENE

AN ARCHWAY PAPERBACK
Published by POCKET BOOKS
New York   London   Toronto   Sydney   Tokyo   Singapore

AN ARCHWAY PAPERBACK *Original*

 An Archway Paperback published by
POCKET BOOKS, a division of Simon & Schuster Inc.
1230 Avenue of the Americas, New York, NY 10020

Copyright © 1990 by Simon & Schuster Inc.
Produced by Mega-Books of New York, Inc.

ISBN: 0-671-70030-8

First Archway Paperback printing November 1990

10 9 8 7 6 5 4 3 2 1

NANCY DREW, AN ARCHWAY PAPERBACK and colophon
are registered trademarks of Simon & Schuster Inc.

THE NANCY DREW FILES is a trademark
of Simon & Schuster Inc.

Cover illustration by Penalve

Printed in the U.S.A.

IL 7+

TRAIL OF LIES

Chapter

One

Hᴀᴠᴇ I ᴛᴏʟᴅ ʏᴏᴜ this is going to be the vacation of a lifetime?" George Fayne asked as the plane began its final descent into Anchorage International Airport. She leaned her dark head against the back of her seat so that her friend could see past her out the window.

"At least a hundred times already!" Nancy Drew retorted. She tossed her reddish blond hair and laughed. "But who's counting?" Outside the small window the craggy peaks of snow-covered mountains sprawled across the land. Soon the city of Anchorage came into view.

"It's beautiful!" George exclaimed.

Carson Drew, Nancy's father, leaned from

1

his seat across the center aisle of the first-class cabin to speak to the two girls. "Henry Wilcox has been telling me that for years. He brags about Alaska almost as much as he does about his son, Steve."

"Right. Steve is just a little older than I. All my life, Dad and Mr. Wilcox have had a competition going over who can tell the most outrageous stories about how great their children are," Nancy told George, with a teasing glance at her father. "Sometimes my ears burn when I hear the things he says about me!"

Carson shrugged, his eyes twinkling. "Well, with me as a father you'd have to be just about perfect, wouldn't you?"

Nancy and George burst out laughing. "So that's where you get your self-confidence!" George said to Nancy. Then she turned to Carson. "Seriously, though, Mr. Drew, I can't thank you enough for inviting me to come along."

"I can't take all the credit," Carson told her. "Henry suggested that Nancy bring a friend."

Two weeks earlier Carson Drew's old friend Henry Wilcox had telephoned, urging Carson to visit him in Alaska. Though Henry and Carson saw each other infrequently, they had kept in touch over the years since they had gone to college together. Now Henry owned a successful shipping firm in Anchorage. Nancy had heard all about it, just as she had heard all about Henry's son's prowess in everything from school to sports.

Nancy and her father tried to take a vacation together every year, but they rarely succeeded. As one of River Heights's prominent attorneys, Carson was frequently tied up in lengthy court cases. And all too often, when Carson was free, Nancy wasn't. Though she was only eighteen, she already had a well-deserved reputation as a detective, and it was rare for her not to be involved in some kind of investigation. When Henry Wilcox's invitation had arrived, though, both Nancy and her father were fortunate to be between cases. It was the chance of a lifetime.

"Be sure to check the overhead compartments for your personal belongings," the flight attendant droned after the airplane landed. The pilot eased the jumbo jet up to the gate, and moments later the three travelers were walking into the sleek, modern terminal building.

They had purposely packed lightly, so they wouldn't have to wait for their luggage at the baggage claim area. "Rental cars this way," Nancy said, seeing a sign directing them to ground services. "Isn't that where Mr. Wilcox is supposed to meet us?"

While Carson Drew looked for Henry Wilcox, Nancy and George wandered to the shops that lined one side of the large terminal.

"Too bad Bess couldn't come, too," George said as they peered into the shop windows. Bess Marvin was George's cousin and also Nancy's close friend. She was visiting relatives in Florida and couldn't join Nancy and George.

"Oh, I'll bet she's having plenty of fun in the sun right now. We ought to take something home for her, though," Nancy suggested. "What about this?" She pointed to a display case in the window of a shop that featured native Alaskan art.

Beautifully carved jade and ivory statues were neatly arranged on glass shelves. The one that had caught Nancy's eye was a tiny puffin made of ivory. The workmanship was so good that the small bird seemed almost alive.

"Let's buy it," George said eagerly.

"You don't have to shop at the airport. All the stores in Anchorage are waiting for you." The unfamiliar voice came from behind the girls.

Nancy turned and saw her father standing next to a tall, thin man with carrot red hair and bright blue eyes.

"Girls, this is John Tilden," Carson introduced them. "He works for Henry."

"Please call me John. I'm Mr. Wilcox's butler and"—John Tilden grinned at the girls—"sometimes his chauffeur. Mr. Wilcox was

4

tied up, so he asked me to drive you out to the house. Can I help with anyone's baggage?"

"Oh, no, we're fine," Nancy assured him. The three of them followed him out to the parking garage.

After the warmth of the plane and the terminal, the air outside felt frigid. Nancy tugged her cap down over her ears. "Brrr. It's really cold here, and it's only November."

When they'd stowed their suitcases in the trunk, John walked to the front of the car. An electrical cord stretched from under the hood to an outlet in a concrete post.

Nancy watched with amazement as the chauffeur unplugged the car. "What's that for?" she asked.

"It's a heater designed to keep the engine from freezing," John explained. "The arctic winters are so cold that cars won't start unless you keep them warm."

"Wow—that's *cold*," George marveled.

"Where is Henry?" Carson Drew asked as they drove out of the airport. John turned the car onto a highway and headed southeast.

"Mr. Wilcox was in Barrow yesterday and didn't get home until late," he replied. "He wanted to finish up some things at the office so he could spend the rest of the week with you."

"That sounds like Henry." Carson nodded. "He's as bad at taking vacations as I am."

"Are those the Chugach Mountains?" Nancy asked, pointing toward the snowcapped range on the horizon ahead of them.

"That's right," John told her. "We're almost home."

They drove along a road with a thick evergreen forest on both sides. A few minutes later, in a clearing, an enormous frame house rose above them. It was three stories high, and its ornate trim told Nancy it had been built during the Victorian era. It would have been a grand house anywhere, but with the rugged Alaskan mountains behind it, it was truly magnificent.

"What a place!" George exclaimed.

"You can say that again!" Nancy agreed.

Just as the car came to a stop in front of the Wilcox home, the front door opened and two very tall men hurried across the front porch. Carson, Nancy, and George climbed out of the car.

"Talk about timing!" the older of the two exclaimed, clapping Carson on the back. "I just got home. Welcome to Alaska."

"It's great to be here," Nancy's father said. He turned to introduce the two girls, but Henry interrupted.

"You're Nancy," he declared. "I'd have known you anywhere—you look just as your father described you. And you must be George." He turned to the young man who stood behind him. "This is my son, Steve."

The introduction was almost unnecessary, for Steve had the same attractively rugged features and tall, lean build that his father did. Henry's brown hair was liberally streaked with gray, but both father and son had the same brown eyes.

"Pleased to meet you," Steve said, staring at George. He gave her a slow smile. "This weekend has just gotten off to a great start."

George flushed with pleasure.

Nancy was about to step forward to greet Steve when he turned and walked to the front door. "Why don't we go inside?" he suggested, holding the door open for George.

Odd, Nancy thought, as she followed them in. It was almost as though Steve hadn't seen her. He must be really dazzled by George! she decided, smiling to herself.

John carried their luggage indoors, and then Henry turned to Carson. "Let's go to my study. We don't want to bore the young people with talk about things that happened before they were born."

Steve Wilcox led the girls into the den, a large, comfortable-looking room paneled with dark wood. There was a fireplace on one wall and a big-screen TV on another. Nancy sank into one of the oversize leather chairs, while George took a seat on the couch.

Steve remained standing. "I've heard a lot about you, Nancy," he said.

Nancy was taken aback. Though Steve's words were harmless, his tone was almost sneering. "All good, I hope," she answered with an attempt at lightness.

"Naturally." Again, Steve's voice had a slightly mocking quality. He sat down at the other end of the couch and faced George. "What would you like to do while you're here?" he asked her. "I'm your tour guide, chauffeur, and whatever else you'd like."

A soft smile crossed George's face. There was no doubt that Steve was attracted to her, and she was obviously enjoying the attention. Nancy wondered if George had missed the hostility Steve seemed to feel for Nancy.

At that moment the doorbell rang, and Steve rose to his feet. "I'd better get that—John's upstairs," he explained, excusing himself and leaving the room. A minute later he returned with a blond man who appeared to be twenty-two or twenty-three.

"This is my friend Craig Miller." Steve introduced the two girls.

Craig was about an inch shorter than Steve, and he had a heavier build. His features were pleasant, though he wasn't as handsome as his friend.

Craig sank into the chair next to Nancy's. "I'm not just a friend—I'm also an employee," he told the girls, but his smile took the sting out of the words. "I'm Steve's dog trainer."

"Sled dogs?" Nancy asked, instantly curious.

"The only kind to have in Alaska." Craig's blue eyes lit up with enthusiasm. Nancy could tell that training dogs was more than a hobby for him.

"Do you race them?" George asked.

Craig gestured toward Steve. "Steve does. He'll be in the Solstice Derby next month."

"I'm going to win it," Steve said confidently. He folded his arms behind his head and lounged back on the couch. "Between my dogs and Craig's training, no one can beat me."

"Lindsay Dunning might disagree with you," Craig commented.

"Who is Lindsay Dunning?" Nancy asked.

"No one to worry about," Steve answered. At the same moment Craig said, "She's Steve's biggest competitor."

George laughed. "Which one of you is right?"

"I am," the two young men replied, again at exactly the same time. This time everyone laughed.

"You don't know how privileged you are to see Craig tonight," Steve told Nancy and George. "Usually he spends the weekend nights training the dogs. He lives in the apartment over our garage just so he can be near them."

Craig turned to Nancy. "Well," he said, "given the choice of spending Saturday evening with the dogs or you . . ."

"You'd pick the dogs," Nancy completed, smiling.

"Not quite," Craig said warmly. He looked at her, his eyes sparkling. Nancy's smile broadened. The tension she had felt earlier was gone, thanks to Craig's easy banter.

Just then the doorbell rang again.

"I'll get it," Craig offered. He stood and left the room. A moment later, they heard voices in the front hall. Then Craig appeared in the doorway. "Steve, where's your father?"

Two men stood behind him. Both wore identical heavy parkas, each with a badge on the left sleeve. Craig looked worried.

"He's in his study," Steve said, standing quickly. "Why?"

"These men are from the police," Craig said. He sounded nervous. "They want to ask your dad some questions!"

Chapter

Two

W HAT'S GOING ON?" Steve demanded.

"Our business is with your father," the shorter of the police officers said.

The other officer looked around. "Will you take us to him?"

His lips set in an angry line, Steve led the two officers to his father's study. When he returned to the den, he walked to the fireplace and poked at the logs with more vigor than necessary.

"Dad wouldn't let me stay," he grumbled.

"Maybe there's a problem at the shipyard," George volunteered. "A break-in or something."

Steve tossed another log on the fire and watched as the sparks flew up the chimney.

11

"Whatever it is, it had better not interfere with my racing in the Solstice," he said fiercely.

Nancy's eyes widened in surprise. "How could it?" she asked him. "The police are probably here about your father's business. What connection could there be to your racing?"

Steve shrugged. "My dad thinks dogsledding is a nice hobby but not a career. He'll use any excuse to get me working back at the shipyard."

George spoke up. "I'm sure he knows how important racing is to you."

"For Dad, nothing's as important as Wilcox Shipping." A frustrated look flitted across Steve's face. "But I'm not going to let anything come between me and winning the Solstice Derby. Not my father, not anything."

The tension in the room crackled almost as loudly as the logs in the fireplace. Then there was a knock at the door.

"Come in, John," Steve called when he saw the man standing in the doorway.

"Your father asked that we delay dinner an hour," the butler explained. "His attorney is on his way over for a meeting, and they think it will take a while."

Though no one said anything, Nancy was sure they were all thinking the same thing she was: Henry Wilcox wouldn't have called his attorney unless the situation was serious.

"Er—would you like to see your room now?" John asked Nancy and George. "There's plenty of time to unpack before dinner, if you'd like to."

"Good idea," George murmured. She and Nancy followed John out to the front hall and upstairs.

The sight of the luxurious room the two girls would stay in made Nancy stop wondering about Henry Wilcox for a moment. "Wow!" she breathed as John shut the door behind them. "Now, *this* would make Bess really jealous!"

"It's gorgeous," George agreed enthusiastically. The walls were a pale shade of peach, and a thick Oriental rug lay on the floor in a rich blaze of colors. Besides the twin canopied beds, there was a sitting area with a fireplace and two comfortable armchairs.

Nancy peeked into the adjoining bathroom. Her eyes widened. "If you think *that's* something, you ought to see this," she called over her shoulder. "There's this great old-fashioned, claw-footed bathtub in here, and it has gold faucets!"

"Wilcox Shipping must make a lot of money," George said. She flopped down on one of the beds.

Nancy nodded and closed the door to the bathroom. "My dad told me Henry Wilcox is a millionaire."

"A millionaire with great taste," George added.

"I'll bet Mrs. Wilcox did the decorating," Nancy replied. "According to Dad she was an interior decorator before she got married. She died when Steve was six."

"Steve is nice, isn't he?" George asked.

Nancy didn't say anything. She wasn't sure she shared George's opinion of Henry Wilcox's son. He had seemed selfish and a little rude to her.

George didn't seem to notice Nancy's silence. "Well, I guess we should unpack," she said.

"Yeah. Now, what did I do with my purse?" Nancy looked around the room. "I guess I left it in the den."

She hurried downstairs. As she went through the hallway, her attention was drawn to a door on the left. It looked like a closet, but it had a window in the door. Nancy realized it was an old-fashioned telephone booth.

John Tilden was inside. As Nancy walked by, he looked up. An expression of surprise flitted across his face. He turned away, cupping his hand around the mouthpiece of the phone as though he didn't want anyone to overhear his words.

Nancy frowned. The glass door of the booth looked thick enough to muffle his voice, yet for some reason John was taking no chances. I wonder why? she thought.

She picked up her purse in the den and went back upstairs to change into some fresh clothes before dinner.

The Wilcox dining room was just as sumptuously decorated as Nancy and George's room. The long table was covered with a fine linen cloth, and the dishes were delicate china.

Unfortunately, no one who was seated at the table seemed able to appreciate the surroundings. Nancy was shocked at the change in Henry Wilcox since the afternoon. He looked gaunt and worried, with a vertical crease between his brows. Concern was etched on Carson Drew's face, too.

"Can you tell us what the police wanted?" Craig asked after John had served their dinner.

The broiled salmon, baked potatoes, and vegetables looked and smelled delicious, and Nancy suddenly realized that she was hungry. Her last meal had been on the plane hours earlier.

"It's pretty straightforward," Henry Wilcox said. "A customs inspector found an illegal shipment of ivory that had apparently been smuggled aboard the *Musk Ox*. That's one of my ships," he added for Nancy and George's benefit.

Craig gripped his fork as though it were a weapon. "I should have been there!" he cried. "I'd have caught the smugglers before they got the stuff onto the ship."

"I don't understand." Nancy was puzzled. "Why should you have been there, Craig?"

"Craig has two jobs. He also works as a night watchman at Wilcox Shipping," Steve explained.

"Yeah," Craig added. "I'm there Monday through Thursday nights. Why did this have to happen on Friday?" He turned back to Henry. "I just wish I'd been at the shipyard. I wouldn't have let it happen."

Henry shook his head slowly. "There was nothing you could have done to stop it, Craig."

"What do you mean?" Nancy asked.

"Someone used the *Musk Ox* to bring elephant ivory into Alaska."

"What's illegal about that?" Steve asked. "We sell lots of ivory in Alaska."

"Native Alaskan walrus ivory," Carson pointed out. "That's legal. But it's illegal to import elephant ivory into the States. The law is designed to help save the elephants from extinction. Poachers kill them for their ivory tusks."

Henry continued. "What they're bringing in are pieces of ivory already carved. Someone's passing them off as genuine Alaskan items."

George looked at Nancy, and Nancy knew

what her friend was thinking. Had the little ivory puffin they'd seen in the airport gift shop been smuggled into Alaska?

"Do the police have any idea who's behind the smuggling?" Nancy asked.

Henry nodded slowly. "They think it's me."

"What?" Steve was shocked.

"The police checked the log, and I was the only person who boarded the ship last night," Henry told him.

"But you're the owner," George protested.

"They think that three in the morning was a strange time for a shipyard visit," Carson explained.

"My trip to Barrow ended late, and I had a lot of work to finish before all of you arrived," Henry continued, "but the police didn't seem to want to listen."

Carson Drew sent his friend an encouraging look across the table. "At least there was no formal accusation, and they've agreed not to make the story public."

"Yet." Henry's tone was grim. "I've spent over twenty years building Wilcox Shipping and making its name synonymous with integrity and service. Now it's being destroyed.

"When people hear about this, they'll never trust me again," he added. "I'm afraid this may ruin my business!"

Chapter

Three

NANCY'S HEART WENT OUT to Henry Wilcox. She knew he was probably right—if he wasn't cleared of the smuggling charges quickly, word would leak out, and his reputation would be ruined in no time. Even if he was eventually proven innocent, his business would suffer severely.

A gloomy silence hung over the table. Looking nervous, John cleared their plates from the table. Then he wheeled a small cart into the dining room, positioning it at the corner of the table between Henry and Nancy. "Dessert will be cherries jubilee," he announced.

"My favorite!" Nancy said, smiling in an attempt to lighten the mood in the room. John began to warm the cherry liqueur in a copper skillet over a small burner. Then he struck a match and held it to the skillet. There was a soft whoosh, and the hot liqueur burst into flame.

At the other end of the table Carson Drew settled back in his chair. "Sorry, Nancy," he said. "I know I promised you a vacation, but it looks like you've got a new case."

Craig turned to Nancy with a puzzled expression on his face. "What does that mean?"

John began deftly spooning hot cherries onto Nancy's dessert plate.

"Nancy's a detective," George put in, answering Craig's question. "Finding out who the smugglers are is right up her alley."

At George's words, John started violently. The skillet rocked, and a tongue of boiling liquid splashed over the side.

Nancy gasped and twitched her arm out of the way. The hot liqueur hit the tablecloth and sizzled for a moment.

"John, be careful!" Henry cried. "Are you all right, Nancy?"

"Yes, I'm fine," Nancy replied, looking sharply at John.

John was pale. "I—I must have lost my grip on the skillet," he said shakily. "I'm so sorry, Miss Drew." He bent down to clean up the mess.

"Well, there's no harm done," Carson said in a soothing tone.

John hurried out of the room. There was a moment of silence, then Craig turned and gave Nancy an appraising look. "So you're a detective, huh?" he said in a skeptical tone.

"That's right," Nancy said. "Mr. Wilcox, if you do want my help on this case, I'll be only too happy to give it."

"I appreciate that," Henry replied. He sounded grateful. "I know from what Carson has told me that you're a brilliant sleuth."

There was a snort from the other end of the table. Startled, Nancy turned and met Steve's scornful gaze. "Terrific. This is just terrific," he growled.

"Hey, Steve, take it easy! I'm sure Nancy will do a great job," Craig said. He reached out and punched his friend lightly on the shoulder.

Steve didn't respond. He just glowered into his dessert plate. What have I done to offend him? Nancy wondered. It really did seem that Steve had some sort of grudge against her.

Maybe it's just that he's worried about his father and he thinks I won't find out anything, Nancy reasoned. But somehow she didn't feel that was the real explanation for Steve's outburst.

Then a thought struck her. Could it be that he was worried about what she *would* find? Did Steve have something to hide?

For that matter, what about John Tilden?

Why had the butler reacted so strongly when he heard she was a detective?

She could find out only by investigating, Nancy knew. "I want to start looking around tonight," she announced. "Is there any way I can get aboard the *Musk Ox?*"

"I'm afraid not. The police have cordoned off the ship until tomorrow morning. No one's allowed on board," Henry said. He cleared his throat and added, "I know Steve and Craig have planned a big night for you and George. Don't change your plans because of this unfortunate situation."

"Hey, that's right!" Craig said enthusiastically. "We wanted to take you to Anchorage's latest night spot. It's called Northern Lights."

"Yes." Steve bent a private smile on George. "It's a great way to get to know Alaska."

"Well, if you're sure you feel up to it . . ." George said, but her dark eyes were shining.

When dinner was over, the girls went upstairs and changed into the party clothes they'd packed. George wore a soft, short-skirted blue knit dress, while Nancy slipped into a bright red top with a matching skirt that swirled around her long legs. George lent Nancy a red silk scarf that her mother had given her. When they came downstairs, Steve and Craig whistled appreciatively.

"Want to take my van?" Steve said to Craig.

"You bet." Craig nodded. "I don't think the girls would like riding in my old truck. It's fine for hauling dogs and supplies, but it's not much for going to a nightclub."

Steve helped George into the front seat of a brand-new van. Craig and Nancy climbed into the back. Nancy noticed that the expensive vehicle had all the options, including a color television.

"Want to watch the news?" Craig asked. "We can see if anyone's leaked the story about the smuggling."

Steve swiveled his head toward the backseat. "No," he said brusquely. Then, as if realizing how harsh he sounded, he said in a softer voice, "Let's not talk about that tonight. We can't do anything about it, anyway."

"Yeah, you're right," Craig agreed. "We want Nancy and George to enjoy their first night in Anchorage. What do you say we give them the scenic tour?"

They drove into the city, retracing the route John had taken from the airport. When they reached the city limits, Steve began pointing out the sights. Anchorage was a bustling city, with fancy hotels, restaurants, and a sprawling downtown area crowded with modern-looking office buildings.

Soon they reached the club. Steve steered the van into a parking spot, and they trooped inside.

"This is fantastic," Nancy said when they were seated at a round table. It was easy to see how the club had gotten its name: the ceiling was covered with flashing colored lights. A band played on the small stage, and the dance floor was crowded with teenagers moving to the pulsing beat of the music.

"The real northern lights are even better," Steve said. He seemed to have thawed a little toward Nancy on the drive in.

"Will we be able to see them while we're here?" George asked.

Nancy thought Steve would answer, but instead he stared at the entrance, his lips curved into a frown. She looked in the direction of his gaze and saw two girls standing in the doorway.

Craig stood up, seemingly unaware of Steve's displeasure. "Come join us," he called, gesturing to the girls and pulling two chairs over from an empty table.

When the girls reached the table, Craig made introductions. "This is Lindsay Dunning," he said after he'd introduced Nancy and George.

Lindsay was tall and had curly, light brown hair. As she slipped off her parka, Nancy could see that she was thin, but she looked strong. For a second Nancy wondered why her name sounded familiar. Then she remembered. Lindsay was Steve's main competition in the upcoming Solstice Derby. That must be why he had frowned when he saw her.

"And this is Amanda Spear," Craig said. A couple of inches shorter than her friend, Amanda had huge gray eyes. Her long blond hair was tucked into a luxurious silver fox jacket.

Amanda and Lindsay said hello, and Lindsay started to take one of the empty chairs.

"Let's not sit here, Lindsay," Amanda said in a voice that carried. "I don't like snakes."

"There aren't any snakes in Alaska," Craig said. His laugh sounded forced.

Amanda didn't laugh. "I was talking about the two-legged variety." She glared at Steve.

"Oh, come on, Amanda." Lindsay tugged at her friend's arm until she reluctantly took the remaining seat. "Let's at least have a soda."

Amanda pulled off her gloves and unfastened her jacket. "It's nice to meet you," she said to Nancy and George, turning so that her back was to Steve.

As though he hadn't noticed Amanda's rudeness, Steve began talking in a low voice to George.

Craig leaned across the table toward Lindsay. "How's the training coming?"

"Great!" Lindsay tossed her head, and her short curls bounced. "I hate to boast, but my team's going to win the Solstice Derby."

Steve looked up sharply. "Oh, yeah?"

Amanda turned around. She smiled sweetly, but there was venom in her eyes. "You don't have a chance, Steve. You never did."

Nancy saw Steve's hand clench into a fist, but he said nothing. Instead he turned to George. "Want to dance?"

"I'd love to." George smiled, her expression relieved. She followed him onto the dance floor.

"How about you?" Craig said to Amanda. "Want to show me what a great dancer you are?"

As the two left the table, Lindsay took a long swallow of the soda the waitress had just brought her. Her eyes were troubled.

"I want to apologize for my friend," she said to Nancy, putting her glass down. "Amanda's not usually so rude. It's just that she and Steve used to date, and she really took it badly when he broke it off. I never thought he'd be here tonight, or we wouldn't have come."

"No need to apologize. I guess she's still pretty upset," Nancy said sympathetically. The situation was awkward, but she was glad to know the reason for the obvious tension between Amanda and Steve.

"You seem excited about your dogs," she said to Lindsay, changing the subject.

A grin of pure pleasure crossed Lindsay's

face. "Racing sled dogs is in my blood. We've all been bitten by the bug—Steve, Craig, and me. Only Amanda has escaped. I tell you, Nancy, once you've driven a team, you're hooked."

Nancy smiled and pushed her reddish blond hair off her shoulders. She'd read about sled-dog races. "It sounds like a lot of fun," she said.

"Have you seen Steve's dogs yet?" Lindsay asked.

Nancy shook her head.

"I'm sure Steve will let you drive his, but if he doesn't, I'll be glad to give you a chance on my team," Lindsay offered.

"Hey, thanks! I may take you up on that," Nancy replied. The song ended, and she looked up as the two couples returned to the table. George looked happy and flushed, and Steve and Craig were both smiling. Only Amanda still seemed glum.

"Want to take your chances with my two left feet?" Craig asked Nancy.

"If you'll risk mine," she quipped, knowing her feet were in no danger of being trampled. She'd seen Craig dancing with Amanda, and he was quite good.

Steve and George stood next to the table, waiting for Nancy to get up. Steve was still holding George's hand.

"Quite the lovebirds," Amanda said sharply.

Steve dropped George's hand as though it had burned him.

"Wow, Steve and Amanda really don't seem to get along," Nancy ventured as she and Craig maneuvered their way onto the crowded dance floor.

"Mmm. Steve's been pretty thin-skinned lately," Craig said in a neutral voice. Then he grabbed Nancy's hand. "But let's not talk about them right now. Let's just have fun, okay?"

Nancy smiled. "Okay."

It was fun being on the dance floor, especially with someone who danced as well as Craig, but for Nancy there was no magic spark. Craig was nice enough, but no one could compare to Ned, her boyfriend back in River Heights.

When the dance ended, she and Craig returned to the table, and Craig ordered everyone another round of sodas. The conversation immediately turned back to sled dogs.

"Have you done your overnight training?" Lindsay asked Steve.

"Nope. Craig's had all the fun," he said.

"Overnight training? What's that?" George asked.

Craig explained that the Solstice Derby involved an overnight stay along the trail. "A lot of the sled-dog races are only one day long," he told them, "but the major ones like the Iditarod involve several nights on the trail. The Solstice Derby is good practice for the big ones."

Amanda was sitting next to Craig. Her blond hair swirled around her shoulders as she turned to him. "Are you still using the cabin?" she asked.

"Sure." Craig nodded. "It's the perfect distance from the kennels. I take a long loop out there to make a full day of running."

Amanda turned back to Nancy and George. "My grandfather and Craig's grandfather were trapping and trading partners when they first came to Alaska," she said. "Times were pretty hard, and they had to share a tiny cabin in the forest north of Anchorage. Craig owns the cabin now."

"It's so romantic up here!" Nancy exclaimed. "Trapping and trading, dogsledding —it's just like those old movies about the far north."

"It's pretty great," Lindsay said with a grin.

The band began a fast song, and Steve and George got up to dance again. Craig followed with Lindsay, leaving Nancy and Amanda at the table.

For a second, Amanda's eyes followed Steve and George. Nancy could see her stiffen with anger. Then she gave Nancy a small smile. "You're lucky to be on vacation. I wish I could get time off."

"Where do you work?" Nancy asked, hoping to get onto a neutral topic of conversation.

Amanda twisted the large gold ring she wore on her right hand. "Wilcox Shipping. I'm the bookkeeper."

Nancy picked up her glass and sipped as she tried to hide her surprise. None of the bookkeepers she knew in River Heights could afford to wear expensive gold rings and fox jackets.

"Lindsay said you're the only one who hasn't caught sled-dog fever," she commented.

Amanda frowned. "I can't afford dogs. They're a very expensive hobby. I don't think anyone makes money racing them. Even the winners just break even."

"A lot of people seem to think racing is more than a hobby," Nancy said. "Steve, for example."

Amanda gave Nancy a sharp glance. "Oh, yeah, Mr. Wonderful." She glanced out at the dance floor, where Steve had just drawn George into his arms. The color drained from her face. For a second Nancy thought she was going to faint.

"Are you okay?" Nancy asked, but Amanda appeared not to hear her.

"Are you okay?" Nancy asked a second time.

Amanda started, as if coming out of a trance. Then she glared at Nancy. "Steve Wilcox is going to regret this evening. I'll make sure of that." With that, she jumped up and strode from the club.

Chapter

Four

T HE SMELL of bacon and eggs wafted up the stairway to the second floor of the Wilcox house the next morning. It was still dark, even though it was after eight.

"Wasn't last night fun?" George asked as she and Nancy dressed. "I really liked Northern Lights. The band was great, and the atmosphere was fantastic. And Steve's such a good dancer!" She grinned. "This is turning out to be one of the best vacations I've ever had."

From the number of superlatives she used, it was obvious George was having a wonderful time. The reason, Nancy suspected, was Steve Wilcox.

"Steve asked me to go skating with him this

morning," George told Nancy as they walked downstairs. "You don't mind, do you?"

"Of course not."

When the two girls entered the dining room they found Carson Drew there alone. A breakfast buffet was set out on the sideboard, with food in warming dishes. A pitcher of juice and pots of tea and coffee were on the long table.

"Where is everybody?" Nancy asked.

"Henry's gone to the shipyard," Carson told her. "And I imagine Steve's still asleep."

Nancy and George piled their plates with fluffy scrambled eggs, hot biscuits, and strips of perfectly fried bacon from the sideboard.

When they were seated, Nancy turned to her father. "I'm glad Mr. Wilcox isn't here, because I wanted to talk to you about him."

George grinned. "That's our Nan. I knew you'd jump into the case first thing this morning."

"What about Henry?" Carson asked.

Nancy spoke slowly. "I know he's your friend, Dad, but do you think he could be involved in the smuggling?"

Carson's reply was adamant. "Absolutely not. Henry Wilcox is honest to a fault. He'd never do anything illegal." Carson gestured with his fork. "You heard him last night. He's worried about his company's reputation. He wouldn't do anything to jeopardize that."

"It's been years since you've seen him," Nancy pointed out. "He might have changed."

Carson shook his head. "Some things don't change. If Henry has a fault, it's that he's too trusting of other people. I could believe he was swindled by some fast-talking person, but I don't believe he's involved in anything illegal."

"It's just that he had the opportunity," Nancy said, swallowing a forkful of eggs. "That's what the police think, and I've got to examine all the possibilities."

"I agree that Henry had opportunity," Carson replied. "But what about motive? You need both."

"Money," Nancy said simply. "There's a lot of money at stake."

"But Mr. Wilcox is a millionaire," George protested. "You told me that."

"His shipping company is very profitable," Carson put in.

"Even the best of businesses can start losing money," Nancy pointed out. "And when they do, the owners may get desperate enough to do something illegal."

"That's all speculation, Nancy," her father told her. "There's no proof."

"I know." Nancy nibbled at a biscuit.

"So what's next?" George asked.

"I'm going to the shipyard," Nancy answered.

Her father reached into his pocket and handed her a set of car keys. "Henry left one of his cars for you to use. Just be careful."

Nancy smiled. "You know I always am." She rose from the table, wiping her lips with her napkin. "If you two will excuse me, I think it's time I got started."

Nancy pulled on her parka and walked briskly to the garage. She took a quick look at a map she found in the glove compartment and then headed into Anchorage.

The morning was clear, and Nancy marveled again at the beauty of the terrain. The sky was streaked with the red of early dawn, those last few minutes before the sun rose.

She glanced at her watch. Nine-thirty. She looked at it again, wondering if it was suddenly running fast. It couldn't be that late, she thought, not with the sun still rising. Then she laughed. This was Alaska, land of the midnight sun! Only now it was nearly winter, and the sun shone for only a few hours a day.

Because it was Sunday, there was little traffic, and soon Nancy was approaching the docks. She parked the car and walked toward the *Musk Ox*.

It was not the largest ship Nancy had ever seen, but it was one of the newest. The exterior was shining with fresh paint, and the ship itself had the sleek lines of recent construction.

Wilcox Shipping had to be doing well to afford a vessel like this.

"Nancy Drew?" the security guard asked when she approached the ship. "Mr. Wilcox told me you'd be coming."

He guided Nancy onto the ship and led the way down a wide flight of stairs. The metal cleats on his boots clacked on the treads. "The cargo's in here," he said, pointing to a huge room filled with pallets that were loaded with boxes.

A stout middle-aged man in a crumpled gray suit stood in the doorway. The guard introduced him as Detective Chandler and explained that Nancy wanted to see how the ivory had been smuggled. "Mr. Wilcox okayed it," the guard added.

Chandler gave the guard a weary look. "What makes Wilcox think he's got any say in a police matter?" he grumbled. But then he beckoned to Nancy. "Okay, I guess it won't hurt if I show you around the place," he muttered. "Let's go."

The guard returned to his post on the upper deck, leaving Nancy and Detective Chandler in the hold.

Nancy looked around at the *Musk Ox*'s cargo. Steel shelving extended from floor to ceiling, lining the four walls and forming long aisles that reminded Nancy of a library's stacks. Only in this case, the shelves were filled with thousands of cartons, rather than with books.

"The customs inspectors found the stuff right here," Detective Chandler told her. He led the way to a pallet of cartons labeled Green Beans. The pile of boxes had been partly unpacked.

"Green beans," Nancy murmured, surprised.

Chandler gestured to another pallet. The stacked cartons were covered with clear plastic wrap. "See, there should have been 192 cartons of beans. But this one had only 191 cartons of beans. The other carton was filled with ivory."

"It looks like it was a middle carton," Nancy said.

"You're right," Chandler agreed. "It's safer that way. When the customs people inspect a pallet, they usually open only the cartons on the edges. This time, by chance, they were a little more thorough."

"Can I see some of the ivory?" Nancy asked.

"Sorry," the detective said. "It was all taken to headquarters as evidence."

Nancy swallowed her disappointment. "Do you know what it looked like?" she asked.

"Little birds," he answered. "Puffins, I think they were."

Like the one she and George had seen at the

airport! "Do you know where the ivory came from?" she asked, excited.

"Sure," Chandler confided. "The ivory's from the Far East. But the beans were loaded onto the ship in Seattle. This smuggling operation is big."

Nancy's mind began to whirl. There had to be at least three people involved. First, there was someone in the Orient who got the ivory to the United States. Then, there was whoever had substituted the carton of ivory for one of beans. That could have occurred either at the food cannery or at the loading dock in Seattle. Finally, there was someone here in Alaska to receive the smuggled goods.

She pulled out a notebook and wrote down the name of the canner, the shipper, and the company in Anchorage that was supposed to receive the beans.

Detective Chandler's beeper suddenly went off. He unclipped it from his belt and looked at the number displayed on it. "Sorry," he said, "but I've got to call the chief." He gave Nancy a long look. "Don't go away—I'll be right back."

Left by herself, Nancy looked around eagerly. This was her chance to search for clues the police might have missed. Spotting a door on the other side of the stairway, she went over and tried it.

It was unlocked. She slipped through it and switched on the lights.

The room, another in the cargo hold, was filled with thousands of cartons. As she walked slowly along the aisles, Nancy looked at the pallets. Everything seemed normal—until she reached the last row. The plastic on one of the pallets was coming loose at one corner.

Nancy pulled out her pocketknife, slit the plastic, and started removing the cartons, which were labeled Cookies. When she reached the center, her probing fingers found a carton that felt heavier than the rest.

Carefully, Nancy eased it out. She slid her knife under the cardboard flaps, loosening the glue so she could open the carton.

Her eyes widened. It was filled with hundreds of ivory carvings.

Nancy unwrapped one of the small figurines and looked at it. Like the puffin she and George had seen in the airport shop, the carving was beautiful. This one was a brown bear standing on its hind legs. Nancy turned it over and noticed a small label with the Alaska state map.

She pulled out her notebook and noted the same data she'd taken from the first pallet. Everything was different—the manufacturer, shipper, and recipient.

Just then, she heard a faint rustling at the other end of the hold.

"I'm over here," she called, expecting to see Detective Chandler.

But the footsteps that approached weren't heavy enough to be Chandler's. And they didn't clack like the guard's. Nancy's scalp prickled.

"Who's there?" she called.

The footsteps stopped. A moment later they started again. But no one answered.

"Who's there?" Nancy demanded again.

Again no answer.

Her heart pounding, Nancy headed for the doorway. Suddenly, the lights went out, and the cargo hold was plunged into utter darkness. A second later, a human form careered into Nancy, knocking her down. Then she heard the door click shut as the mysterious intruder escaped.

Chapter

Five

NANCY SAT UP, groaning a little as she rubbed a bruised elbow. She reached into the pocket of her parka for her penlight. She switched it on, but it was too late. Rapid footsteps climbed the stairs. Whoever had been in the cargo hold had already fled. Turning off the lights had given him the head start he needed to escape without Nancy's seeing him.

She raced up the stairs and looked around the deck. There was no one in sight, not even the security guard. Nancy walked quickly to the other side of the ship, hoping to spot either the guard or the detective.

"Finished, Miss Drew?" the guard asked.

"Just about," Nancy called. "By the way, did anyone else come on board?"

The guard shook his head. "No one."

Detective Chandler came out of the cabin, looking irritated. "Ready to leave?" he asked.

Nancy nodded. It was obvious neither of the men knew about the person in the cargo hold. By now the intruder was safely off the ship, and they'd never catch him. Was it worth mentioning the incident? Probably not—Chandler seemed grouchy enough already.

She told him what she'd found in the second section of the hold. Chandler went back inside the ship's cabin to alert the customs inspectors.

Nancy walked down the gangplank and hurried to the parking lot. It was almost empty. There was a small truck with a security company logo on its door, Nancy's car, and a van—Steve's van.

Nancy's eyes narrowed thoughtfully. Why was Steve at the shipyard this morning? According to George, he had had other plans.

"If it isn't the great investigator." Steve walked around the van from the other side. Despite his flippant words, he seemed startled to see Nancy.

"Hello," she said pleasantly. "I'm surprised you're here. I thought you and George were going skating this morning."

"That was the plan," Steve told her. "But Craig's truck broke down, so I gave him a ride in here to pick up some supplies."

"Did you see the guard when you were on the ship?" Nancy asked.

Steve frowned. "What makes you think I was on the ship?" He gestured to a building in the direction from which he'd come. "Craig and I were in that warehouse." He glared at Nancy as though challenging her to dispute him.

"Nancy!" Craig's voice was warm and friendly. "I didn't expect to see you here."

She turned, glad to see a smiling face. Craig's arms were wrapped around a large carton. Judging from the way he was holding it, it was heavy. As he slid it into the back of the van, he explained, "These are vitamins for the dogs. We buy a lot of stuff by the case right from the suppliers. It's cheaper that way."

"Yeah," Steve mocked. "It's one of the great privileges of being part of the Wilcox empire."

He climbed into the van and roared out of the lot. Nancy walked back to her car. Could Steve have been the intruder in the hold? Or Craig? Steve's reaction to her questions had certainly been violent, but then he seemed to have strong reactions to many things. It was hard to say.

Frowning, she drove back to the Wilcox house.

Steve and Craig were already there when Nancy arrived, and Steve seemed to have gotten over his anger. He was smiling and pleasant all through lunch, and as soon as it was over, he and Craig invited Nancy and George to see the sled dogs.

"I've just been waiting for you to ask," George told Steve as they pulled on their coats. "I'm dying to try dogsledding!"

They trooped outside to a large barn about a hundred yards behind the house. As soon as Steve and Craig walked inside, the dogs began yapping and howling with excitement.

"They're beautiful!" George exclaimed as she knelt to pet two Siberian huskies. "What are their names?"

Steve hunkered down next to her and touched one dog's nose. "This is Thunder," he said softly. "The other dog is Lightning."

Nancy stroked Lightning's head. George wasn't exaggerating. The dogs were among the handsomest she'd ever seen.

"They know we're going to take them for a run," Craig explained, "and they just can't wait."

When he pulled a harness from the wall, the barking intensified. For the next few minutes there was pandemonium as Craig and Steve fitted the harnesses and leashed the dogs to the sled outside.

When all eight dogs were ready, Steve stood

at the back of the sled and released the brake. "Hike!" he yelled. The sled shot forward over the snow. The dogs were suddenly silent as they concentrated on pulling the load.

Craig watched them with a critical eye. "Thunder's a little slow today," he said. "I'll have to give him more vitamins."

As the dog team ran out of sight, Craig turned toward the barn. "Want to help me?" he asked Nancy and George.

Though the barn provided protection against the wind, the dogs did not sleep on the concrete floor. Instead, each had a wooden pallet covered with straw. After Craig had cleaned out the old straw, he dragged a fresh bale from one corner of the barn and started forking it onto the pallets. "This keeps them warm and helps conserve energy," he explained. "That's important in the winter."

Nancy and George grabbed shovels and helped Craig prepare the dogs' beds.

"Thanks," Craig said when they'd finished. "It goes a lot faster when you have help."

"Doesn't Steve help?" Nancy asked.

Craig shook his head. "Steve races the dogs. The care and feeding are up to me."

Nancy thought there was a tinge of resentment in Craig's voice. She was glad when George changed the subject.

"What do you feed the dogs?" she asked.

"Dog food—what else?" Craig laughed.

"We give them the dry stuff in the summer." He gestured toward a fenced-in corner of the barn where several dozen large bags of food were stacked. "During racing season they get hot food, things like cooked meat and fish. Lots of vitamins, too. They burn up a lot of calories running."

The sound of barking told the girls that Steve and the dog team were returning.

"They're in great shape today," Steve said, entering the barn. His face was red with exertion, but he was grinning. For the first time since Nancy had met him, he looked completely happy. "I know I'm going to win the Solstice."

"I hope you do." George smiled at him.

"Want to take them for a run?" Steve offered.

"Could I?" George asked enthusiastically.

"It's easy," Craig assured her, leading them outside. "The dogs are used to running one route here, and they'll go that way. All you have to do is guide them." He pointed to the handlebar. "You hold this and yell when you want the dogs to turn or stop."

"Do you know the commands?" Steve asked.

George shook her head slightly. "I thought everyone said *mush* to get them started, but you yelled *hike.*"

"Everybody uses something different at the

beginning. What's important are *whoa, gee,* and *haw,"* Craig explained. "You know what those mean, don't you? 'Stop,' 'right,' and 'left.'"

George nodded.

"You can ride the runners," Steve said, pointing to the back of the sled. "The only time you have to get off is going up a hill. Then you run behind the sled."

"And you said it was easy." George took her position behind the team, grabbed the handlebar, and released the brake.

"Hike, Thunder!" she cried.

With a jerk, the team was off. Soon George and the dogs disappeared up the trail.

When they came back a short time later, she was grinning from ear to ear. "It's wonderful! Almost like flying!"

Craig checked the dogs and tightened one of the neck lines. "Your turn, Nancy," he said.

Nancy stepped up, grabbed the handlebar, and released the brake. "Hike!" she called.

The dogs surged forward, easily pulling the heavy sled. Thunder, the lead dog, turned his head, as though checking the other dogs' progress, and Nancy heard him bark a short command. In response one of the two wheel dogs, the ones closest to the sled, moved away from his partner.

"Gee!" Nancy shouted the command to turn right as the trail curved. Thunder led the team around the corner. The cold wind drew tears from Nancy's eyes, but she barely noticed. Her pulse was pounding with exhilaration.

All too soon the barn was in sight again, and Nancy had to stop the team with a loud "Whoa!"

"You and George were great!" Craig said enthusiastically. "You're natural mushers."

Nancy laughed, breathless with delight. Lindsay was right. One taste of racing a dog sled, and she was hooked.

"We're going to practice at the local track," Craig said. "Do you two want to come along?"

"Try to keep me away!" George challenged.

The girls helped Steve and Craig load the dogs and the sled into the back of Craig's truck.

"You'd better bring your van, just in case," Craig told Steve. "The truck's running now, but I don't guarantee it."

Steve invited George to ride with him, and it was clear he wanted to be alone with her, so Nancy climbed into the rickety old truck with Craig.

The drive to the track took only a few minutes. When they pulled into the parking lot, Craig groaned. "Uh-oh, trouble. Steve's not going to be too happy about this." He climbed out of the truck and slammed the door. Nancy got out on her side and came around the back of the truck.

Not far away Amanda and Lindsay were busily unloading a team of dogs from a utility van. Though Lindsay was dressed in a practical navy blue parka with heavy down stuffing, Amanda wore ski pants and a hooded jacket made of beaver fur. They soon spotted the new arrivals.

"Oh, look, it's the great Steven Wilcox," Amanda said loudly as Steve got out of his van and went over to help Craig. She straightened, calling after him, "It won't do you any good to practice, you know. You don't have a chance of winning the Derby."

Steve kept his head bent over the dogs' harnesses and remained silent.

"Anyone who treats dogs the way you do deserves to lose," Amanda taunted him.

This time Steve raised his head. Nancy saw his lips thin in anger. Amanda's words had hit their mark.

He still didn't respond, though. He turned to George. "Want a ride on the sled?" he offered. Nancy wondered if that was his way of goading Amanda. She hoped Steve wasn't just using George to make his former girlfriend jealous.

George agreed, casting a sidelong glance at Nancy, then helped Craig and Steve unload the sled. With their team harnessed, Lindsay and Amanda moved to the other side of the track.

"You two don't need to hang around—

George and I can bring the dogs back," Steve said, pointedly dismissing Craig and Nancy. He reached into his pocket and handed Craig his key ring. "Why don't you take the van?"

"Sure thing," Craig said quickly. Nancy was taken aback—she had thought they'd stay to watch Steve practice. She said nothing, though, as she and Craig walked back to the van. Craig unlocked the door and let Nancy in first.

"This is luxury!" Craig said, climbing in the other side. He switched on the engine. "I wish I could afford one."

Nancy settled back in her plush seat. "Your truck is more practical," she pointed out.

"That's true." Then Craig changed the subject. "It sure looks like Steve's interested in George."

"I think it's mutual," Nancy told him.

"I thought they wanted some time together, so I didn't say anything when Steve got rid of us," he said. "I hope you weren't offended. Steve doesn't mean any harm, but he can be tactless sometimes."

"You're a good friend to him," Nancy said. She paused for a second. "Craig, what did Amanda mean when she said Steve mistreated the dogs?"

Craig's voice was harsh. "She spends too much time with Lindsay Dunning, and Lindsay's a fanatic about her dogs. She really coddles those animals. She won't have whips anywhere near them, and she even sings to them when she's out on the trail." Craig steered the van onto the main road. "It drives me crazy listening to Lindsay singing 'This Land Is Your Land' at the top of her lungs at every race."

"Do you use whips?" Nancy asked.

Craig gave her a reassuring smile. "Don't get me wrong. We never beat our dogs. No good musher would mistreat his animals. But we used to do what some of the great Iditarod racers do—we'd crack a whip in the air. It excites the dogs and makes them run faster."

Craig took a sharp curve on the road, then spoke again. "Lindsay made such a fuss that we stopped using the whips. But Amanda doesn't miss a chance to goad Steve about anything."

A few minutes later, the van pulled into the Wilcox driveway. A truck Nancy hadn't seen before was parked in front of the porch. John Tilden and a strange man stood on the porch, talking. The man handed John an envelope.

As the van crunched over the driveway, John's head shot up. He quickly unzipped his parka and thrust the envelope inside. The man he was speaking to jumped into the truck and drove away.

Then, without a glance in Nancy and Craig's direction, the butler slipped inside the house.

Chapter

Six

"I WONDER WHAT John's hiding now," Craig muttered angrily.

"What do you mean, 'now'?" Nancy asked.

Craig flushed slightly. "Nothing. I was just shooting off my mouth." He opened the door and climbed out of the van.

Nancy wasn't convinced. "Come on, Craig. You must have meant something."

For a moment, Craig said nothing. Then, as they walked toward the house, he asked, "Have you ever had a feeling that something's just not right?"

"Sure," Nancy said.

"Well, that's the way I feel about John. I can't put my finger on it, but something's

51

wrong about him. For one thing, he hasn't been with the Wilcoxes very long, and he won't say where he was before that."

Nancy was thoughtful. It wouldn't hurt to ask Henry Wilcox a few questions about his butler.

"Dogsledding is the most exciting thing I've ever tried," George announced at dinner that night.

"It's a truly Alaskan hobby," Henry Wilcox said, emphasizing the word *hobby*. Nancy saw Steve roll his eyes.

"Well, all I know is, it was wonderful!" George said. Her eyes glowed with enthusiasm, and Steve grinned at her.

"Maybe now you'll agree to stay after Nancy and Mr. Drew leave," he suggested.

Carson looked down the table at Henry. "I wish we could spend more than a week here."

"So do I," Henry said, "but I have to admit that my motives are selfish. Now that I have the police breathing down my neck, I'm hoping Nancy will uncover something." He turned to Nancy, his expression serious. "How are you doing with the investigation?"

Nancy shook her head slowly, wishing she had better news. "Not too well, so far." She told them about the second shipment of ivory she had discovered, leaving out the part about the intruder who had turned out the lights. "I've got a couple of leads to check tomorrow when businesses are open again. I want to look at some of the shipping records, too," she concluded.

"I'll have everything ready for you. I hope it helps." Henry looked grim. "The police are giving me only two more days before they break the news to the press. I guess I've been lucky that they agreed to keep it quiet this long."

"You know, they don't have any real evidence against you," Carson said.

"That's what I like," Henry said with a smile that looked forced. "A vote of confidence."

"Henry, there's no way the charges against you will hold up," Craig said firmly. "They're ridiculous. I'm sure the police will catch the real culprit soon. Now, what can we do to make sure these people enjoy Alaska while they're here?"

"Do you think we'll get to see the northern lights?" Nancy asked, taking his cue and changing the subject.

"Well, it's not the best time of year, but there's still a pretty good chance," Craig answered, reaching for more roast beef.

"If you do, be sure to whistle," Steve said.

"Whistle? Why?" George looked puzzled.

"It's an old Eskimo legend," Craig explained. "If you whistle, the lights will dance faster."

"Dancing lights—now I've really got to see them," George said.

Nancy was intrigued. "Where did you hear this legend?"

"My grandpa used to spend time in the Inuit villages when he was trapping and trading," Craig explained. "He learned a lot from the people, and not just stories about the northern lights."

When dinner was over, Nancy suggested they all go outside to look for the northern lights.

"Sorry," Steve said, "but I've had enough exercise for one day. I'm beat!"

"Better count me out, too," Craig said.

"Wimps," Nancy teased. She and George grabbed their heavy coats out of the foyer closet, then went outside.

Nancy looked up at the sky. It was a clear, moonless night. "Let's get away from the house lights," she suggested. "We'll be able to see better."

They walked for a few minutes until they were in the forest. It was completely dark and bitterly cold. Nancy could feel the breath freezing in her nostrils.

"Will we know the northern lights if we see them?" George asked.

"I don't think we'll be able to miss them."

They continued walking, clutching each other's mittened hands so they wouldn't get separated in the darkness, but they saw nothing. They were almost ready to call it quits when it happened.

They came to a clearing, and Nancy gasped in wonder. Bands of blue and green shot across the sky, followed by brilliant reds and yellows that seemed so close Nancy almost reached out to try to touch them.

"Whistle!" she said to George.

Both of them pursed their lips and began to whistle. The colored bands pulsed and shifted. George let out a laugh of pure delight. The lights really did seem to dance in time with the whistling!

Gradually the display began to fade. When the last light had dimmed, George said softly, "That was great."

A grin spread across Nancy's face. "I'll never, ever forget it."

She and George were quiet as they walked back to the house, awed by the incredible natural spectacle they'd just seen. It was only when they were out of the forest that George spoke again.

"I'm so glad you asked me to come to Alaska with you," she said. "Not just because of the northern lights, either." She was silent for a moment. Nancy sensed her hesitation.

"I really like Steve," George said finally. "He's a lot of fun."

Nancy's reply was sincere. "I'm glad for you, George. Steve seems to like you, too."

"But not *you,*" George said, voicing Nancy's unspoken thoughts.

"You could say that," Nancy said mildly.

George stopped and faced Nancy. "It bothers me, Nan. I don't think Steve's normally so rude—I don't think I could like him as much if he was really like that. This afternoon I asked him why he's so cold to you, but he wouldn't give me a reason. He said I was imagining it."

Nancy heard the hurt in George's voice and tried to soothe her. "Maybe it's just chemistry," she suggested. "We didn't hit it off from the beginning. But I don't think it's anything to worry about. I can take it."

"I don't know." George sounded miserable. "I just wish I knew what the problem was."

Me, too, Nancy thought to herself.

They climbed the porch stairs and let themselves in the front door of the house. The dining room was empty, and there was no sign of Carson, Henry, Craig, or Steve.

"I wonder where the guys are," George said.

Just then, loud voices carried through the door of the den.

"Calm down, Steve!" Craig's voice said.

Steve's voice was anything but calm. "I don't care what you say," he shouted. "I don't want Nancy Drew here. She'll mess up everything!"

Chapter

Seven

THE DOOR of the den flew open, and Steve stormed into the hallway. At the sight of the girls, his face flushed red with embarrassment.

"I think you owe Nancy—" George started to say.

Nancy quickly shushed her. If Steve made an apology, she wanted it to be because he decided to, not because George shamed him into it.

"Good night, George," Steve said stiffly. He headed for the stairs without even acknowledging Nancy's presence.

"Steve!" George started to follow him, but the look he gave her stopped her in her tracks.

"You could call that bad chemistry," Nancy

said with an attempt at humor after Steve had disappeared.

"More like bad manners," George countered glumly. "I just don't understand him."

Craig came to the door of the den.

"Can I talk to you, Nancy?" he asked quietly.

George flashed Nancy a smile. "I'm off to bed," she murmured, then started up the stairs.

"What is it, Craig?" Nancy asked, walking into the den. Craig motioned her to a chair, but she remained standing.

"I—I just want to apologize for Steve," he said. "His manners have been atrocious. But believe me, that's not the real Steve."

Nancy bit her tongue. It was the only Steve she'd seen.

"He's not himself," Craig continued. "He's awfully upset about the smuggling and what the charges could mean to his father. I guess the strain has made him snap at everyone around him."

Privately, Nancy didn't think Steve had shown all that much concern about his father's troubles, but she wasn't going to argue with Craig. "It's a tough situation," she said neutrally. "Look, Craig, don't worry about me. If Steve has something against me, that's his problem. There's nothing any of us can do about it." Stifling a yawn with her hand, she added, "Now, I've got to get to bed before I fall asleep on my feet."

That wasn't strictly true. Nancy needed to be alone so she could think about what she'd just heard. What had Steve meant by saying she would "mess up everything"?

What did Steve have to fear from Nancy? His outburst made no sense whatsoever— unless he was the smuggler. Then he would have reason to fear Nancy, because she might uncover his scheme.

It was a great theory, except for one thing: from what she had seen in the past day, Steve Wilcox had everything money could buy. He apparently had no motive to smuggle!

As she drove to the Wilcox Shipping offices the next morning, Nancy couldn't help feeling happy. No matter how little progress she had made on the case, it was a beautiful day. Once again, the dark sky was clear, with a reddish tint in the east that meant the sun was going to rise soon. Before she reached downtown Anchorage, the fiery red ball had climbed over the Chugach Mountains.

She gazed in wonder at one peak, soaring above the others. At first she'd thought it was a cloud, hovering on top of the mountains. Then she realized the huge mass of white was a snow-covered mountain—Mount McKinley. No wonder the Inuits called it the Great One! It was so tall it dwarfed the rest of the range. Nancy wondered whether George could see McKinley from wherever she and Steve were training the dogs. She hoped so.

The shipping offices were located on Anchorage's main street, Fourth Avenue. Nancy had no trouble finding the building. She parked and went in, taking the stairs to the second floor offices.

"Is Mr. Wilcox here?" Nancy asked the receptionist. She gazed around curiously. Like Henry Wilcox's house, the Wilcox Shipping offices were attractively decorated and exuded an air of prosperity.

"I'm sorry, but he was called away." The woman gave Nancy an appraising look. "Are you Nancy Drew?"

At Nancy's nod, the receptionist told her, "Mr. Wilcox said Amanda Spear could help you. Third cubicle on the right."

Nancy felt a momentary frustration. She'd wanted to talk to Henry about John's previous employer. Now she'd have to wait.

"Good morning," she said as she poked her head into Amanda's cubicle.

Amanda was seated at a large desk staring intently at a computer screen. She started at Nancy's voice, then smiled nervously. "Hi."

Nancy took one of the visitors' chairs. "I was hoping to talk to you at the track yesterday," she said.

"Too bad you didn't stay. Lindsay trounced Steve." There was no hiding the satisfaction in Amanda's voice.

Nancy looked around the cubicle. Other than a nice desk clock, there were no personal possessions, none of the usual pictures and knickknacks that told a lot about the person who worked in an office. The only thing that appeared to belong to Amanda was the fox jacket she'd worn the other night. It was hanging from a hook in one corner.

"Did Mr. Wilcox tell you I was coming?" Nancy asked.

Amanda unclasped her hands and began to twist the huge gold ring on her right hand. "Yes. He says you're a detective," she said. Her voice quavered ever so slightly. "You're the first one I've met."

Nancy smiled. "I hope you're not disappointed—I'm not wearing a trench coat or carrying a magnifying glass or anything." She wanted to put Amanda at ease. The young woman was obviously nervous about this visit. Why was that?

"So what are you investigating?" Amanda twisted her ring again and glanced at the clock.

Nancy and Henry had agreed last night that it was best not to tell the company's employees about the smuggling. "Oh, I'm just helping Mr. Wilcox out with a little problem," Nancy said vaguely. "I'd like to take a look at the shipping records and the company financial statements."

Was it Nancy's imagination, or did Amanda grow a shade paler at her request?

"Oh—sure. Let me set you up," Amanda said quickly. She led the way to an empty cubicle. "You can work in here—no one will bother you. I'll get the books."

A few minutes later she returned with three large binders, which she deposited in front of Nancy. Thanking her, Nancy pulled out a calculator and a pad of paper and got to work.

As she looked through the company's financial information, Nancy began to wish she knew more about accounting. Everything looked in order to her, but she was having a hard time following all the columns of debits and credits. She flipped to the payroll but soon gave up—that was even more confusing.

One thing seemed certain from these accounts, however: Wilcox Shipping was indeed a very prosperous company. The numbers at the bottom of each column showed clear profits. Nancy was glad. The case against her father's friend was looking weaker, since he had no obvious motive to smuggle.

Nancy pulled out the shipping records to look at the cargo list for the *Musk Ox*'s last trip. She studied the sheets for the shipments of beans and cookies. They showed the same information she'd seen stenciled on the outside of the cartons. The packers for each were different. So were the companies who were supposed to receive the food.

The *Musk Ox* had stopped in four ports to pick up cargo, she noted. Where had Detective Chandler said the beans were picked up? She looked at the sheet again. Seattle. And the cookies?

Aha! A smile of satisfaction spread across Nancy's face. The cookies had come from Seattle, too. So both pallets with ivory in them had been loaded there. It was the first link she'd found.

Eagerly she searched through the manifest, looking for other cargo that had been loaded in Seattle. There was only one other entry—three pallets of paperback books. If her theory was correct, one of those pallets might contain a carton of carved ivory figurines rather than books.

There was only one way to find out. But first she had one more binder of company records to search. She started looking through the personnel records for Wilcox Shipping. Her eyes widened in surprise at an unexpected name on the employee roster: Steven Wilcox.

Now, why didn't anyone mention to me that Steve worked at his father's company? Nancy thought. She skimmed through his file. Steve had worked in accounting, like Amanda. He had quit without notice six weeks ago. According to the books, he had resigned, but no reason was given.

Was there any significance in the date? Or in the fact that Steve and Amanda had worked together? Nancy resolved to question Amanda as soon as she was done with the books.

Craig's records appeared to be in order. He normally worked four days a week, as he'd said, with an occasional night or two of overtime. Nothing unusual there.

Finally, Nancy checked Amanda's salary. She earned a modest amount. It was enough to afford a nice apartment if she had a roommate, but Nancy could see no way Amanda's salary could stretch to afford two fur coats and a huge gold ring.

Unless Amanda had another source of income.

Suddenly Nancy was very interested in the bookkeeper. Amanda's evident alarm when Nancy had asked to see the books, combined with her obviously extravagant life-style, suggested that she was up to something. Was it something illegal? Something to do with smuggling ivory aboard her employer's ships?

Yes, it was time to talk to Amanda.

Nancy walked back to Amanda's cubicle, but it was empty. The fox jacket was no longer hanging on its hook. "You just missed her," the girl across the aisle called. "If you hurry, you might catch her at the elevator."

Nancy grabbed her coat and sprinted out of the office. Amanda wasn't in the hallway. Nancy saw that the elevator was way up at the top floor. There had to be a stairway. She looked down the hallway and saw a red exit sign at the far end.

Nancy ran, pushed open the door, and started down the stairs. Her boots clattered on the cement and echoed in the stairwell.

Suddenly a tremendous force hit her from behind, pushing her off balance. Her arms flailed wildly, but it was no use.

In a moment, she was tumbling down the stairs head over heels!

Chapter

Eight

JUST BEFORE SHE HIT the cement landing, Nancy twisted her body sideways, tucked her head, and flung her arms out to absorb the shock.

She landed with a thud and lay there for a moment, stunned. Then, gingerly, she moved her arms and legs. Nothing seemed to be broken.

Groaning slightly, she reached up and felt her head. It was still there. She was thankful she'd learned how to fall properly in her martial arts classes. Though she was going to be badly bruised, she had no serious injuries.

Nancy stood up and gazed at the stairwell. She saw no one, but there was no doubt in her mind that someone had pushed her.

Amanda knew I was here, Nancy thought. She shivered. Would Amanda have the strength—or the nerve—to push someone down the stairs? It was impossible to say.

Nancy took a few moments to catch her breath and smooth her clothes. Then she went back to the Wilcox Shipping offices. There she spotted two familiar faces by the receptionist's desk.

"John, Craig! I didn't know you were going to be here!" Nancy exclaimed.

Craig greeted her. "There was a mix-up with my overtime pay on Friday, so Mr. Wilcox said he'd have another check ready for me this morning." He grinned. "You know what it's like when you've spent the check before you get it."

"I wish I'd known you were coming here, Craig," John Tilden put in. "You could have saved me a trip. Mr. Wilcox asked me to bring some papers back to the house."

"Has anyone seen Amanda Spear?" Nancy asked.

Both Craig and John shook their heads.

Nancy stuck her head into Amanda's cubicle. It was just the way she'd left it a few minutes earlier, and there was no sign of the bookkeeper.

"Want a ride back to the house?" Craig offered.

Nancy shook her head. "I've got the other

car here," she explained. "And I still have a couple of errands to run."

She said goodbye to the two men, then went to the hall and pushed the button for the elevator. One trip down the stairs was enough for the day!

When she stepped outside, Nancy looked for a pay phone. She wanted to call her father, to see if he knew where Henry was. Then she planned to go to the *Musk Ox* to search the shipment of paperback books.

"Wait up, Nancy!" a voice called.

Nancy turned. Lindsay Dunning was a few yards away, waving and hurrying in Nancy's direction.

"Brrr," Lindsay said, shivering. "I've lived here since I was little, and the cold still gets to me. Want to have a cup of cocoa? The coffee shop here makes the best in the city."

"Sounds good to me." Nancy was glad for the chance to talk to Lindsay.

The two girls went inside and sat at a table. "Are you coming to the sled-dog trials tomorrow?" Lindsay asked when the waitress set two cups of steaming cocoa in front of them.

"Absolutely," Nancy promised. "I can't wait. From what George said, it's almost as exciting as a real race."

Lindsay took a sip of her cocoa. "George looks like she's a dogsledding convert."

"She's not the only one," Nancy admitted,

her blue eyes sparkling. "Steve let me take the team on a short run, and it was great. You were right—one try and you're hooked."

Nancy scooped the whipped cream off the top of her cocoa and ate it. This was her opportunity to turn the conversation to Amanda.

"It's strange that only Amanda seems immune to dogsledding fever."

Lindsay frowned and sipped her cocoa again. "She was never a big fan, but it's only since she and Steve broke up that she seems to hate it."

"Was that a long time ago?"

Lindsay shook her head. "Maybe five or six weeks ago. It was sudden—Amanda had no idea it was going to happen."

Six weeks, Nancy thought. It had also been six weeks since Steve had quit his job at Wilcox Shipping.

"Amanda and Steve used to work together, didn't they?" she asked.

"That's right," Lindsay told her. "Amanda loved it, because she got to see Steve every day."

"I wonder why he quit his job. Do you know?"

"No." Lindsay shook her head. "He never said. But I think maybe something happened. He's been pretty unpleasant ever since. I don't know what's gotten into him."

Hmm. So, six weeks ago, something had happened to make Steve quit his job, break up with his girlfriend, and become generally bad-tempered. Well, at least that told Nancy she had been right to disagree with Craig. Whatever was wrong with Steve, it had little to do with his father's impending legal troubles.

Nancy glanced at her watch. "I was hoping to meet Amanda for lunch, but she left before I could ask her. Do you have any idea where she usually goes at lunchtime?"

Lindsay shrugged. "Sorry. I'm not normally in town for lunch. This time of year, training the dogs is pretty much a full-time job. I just came in today to do some shopping."

When they'd finished their cocoa, the two girls paid the waitress and walked outside. Nancy's eye caught the colorful sign of a craft store across the street.

"Is that a good shop?" Nancy asked. The store was called the Totem Pole.

"If you want real Alaskan crafts, it's the best," Lindsay told her.

"I wanted a Christmas present for my friend Bess," Nancy explained. "I thought it would be nice to give her something from Alaska."

Lindsay needed no more encouragement. "I love to shop. Let's go!" she said, grinning at Nancy. During the next break in traffic, they darted across the street.

The windows of the Totem Pole were filled

with displays of gold-nugget jewelry, beaded mukluks, painted wooden masks, and soapstone carvings. It was the shelves of carved ivory inside the shop that drew Nancy's attention, however.

The girls went inside. "May I look at some of these?" Nancy asked the shopkeeper, pointing at the figurines.

The shopkeeper pulled out a tray of carvings. "This is a particularly nice piece," she said, holding up a moose for Nancy's consideration.

The artist had done a superb job of capturing the awkward majesty of the moose, but it wasn't the piece Nancy wanted. She looked at the tray again, as though considering. Then she pointed to one statue.

"I'd like to see that one," she said. It was a brown bear standing on its hind legs. If Nancy wasn't mistaken, it was identical to the one she'd found on the *Musk Ox.*

"I prefer the moose myself, but this is a nice piece," the shopkeeper said as she handed the bear to Nancy. "We just got it about a month ago."

Nancy held the small bear in her hand, touching the intricate carving. The weight was about the same as the one on the *Musk Ox,* and the carving looked identical. She knew the bear couldn't have come from the *Musk Ox,* because nothing had been unloaded from the ship.

But what if it wasn't the first time ivory had been brought into Alaska on one of the Wilcox ships? The bear could have been part of an earlier smuggled shipment.

"Turn it over," the shopkeeper urged Nancy. "See the label with the state map on it? That's your assurance that it's a genuine Alaskan handicraft. No one except Alaskan artisans can use it."

It was the same label Nancy had seen on the bears in the *Musk Ox*. Whoever was smuggling in the ivory was also counterfeiting the Alaska label.

Nancy looked at the other ivory pieces for a few minutes longer, pretending to be considering them. Then she pointed to the bear. "I'll take that one," she said.

Nancy handed the storekeeper some money. While they waited for her to ring up the sale, Lindsay remarked, "I liked the moose better, too. There was something—I don't know— more genuine about it, I thought."

You don't know how right you might be, Lindsay! Nancy was thinking. But she just smiled and said nothing.

The girls thrust their hands into their mittens as they left the store. "Where next?" Lindsay asked.

Nancy looked down the street, considering the signs. She wanted to find another craft store to see whether it had the same bears for sale. There didn't appear to be another nearby, though.

She looked idly at the stores across the street, and then did a double take. Amanda was coming out of a jewelry store. There was no mistaking the fox jacket or the long blond hair that streamed over it.

"Amanda!" Nancy cried.

The girl swiveled at the sound of Nancy's voice. For a second she stared into Nancy's eyes. Then she turned abruptly and started walking in the other direction.

"Amanda!" Nancy called again.

Amanda's step quickened.

"She must not have seen us," Lindsay said, looking across the street at her friend. But Nancy knew that wasn't true. Amanda had seen her and deliberately gone the other way.

The traffic light turned to green, and a stream of cars filled the street. There was no break in the traffic and no way Nancy could run across the street.

"Wait!" she called.

But Amanda didn't wait. She disappeared through the revolving door of a large building half a block away.

"Let's go!"

Lindsay was one step behind Nancy as traffic

stopped. The two girls raced across the street and down the sidewalk to the building where they'd last seen Amanda. They pushed the revolving door and found themselves in the lobby of an apartment building.

There was no sign of Amanda.

"Is this where Amanda lives?" Nancy asked.

Lindsay's expression was thoroughly puzzled. "No, her apartment's out near Fort Richardson."

"Can I help you ladies?" a uniformed guard asked.

"We're looking for a friend," Nancy explained. "A pretty girl with blond hair and a silver fox jacket."

The guard shook his head. "Haven't seen her."

"But we saw her come in this door," Lindsay insisted.

"I would have remembered someone like that," the guard said, shrugging. "Sorry. Maybe she went into another building."

Nancy's lips tightened in frustration. She was positive now that Amanda was hiding something from her. At that moment, the girl was definitely at the top of Nancy's suspect list. But how was she going to get to the truth, when her prime suspect had just vanished into thin air?

Chapter

Nine

"THAT'S WEIRD," Lindsay said. The two girls
went back out to the street. "I wonder where
Amanda could have gone?"

"Maybe the guard was busy and just missed
seeing her," Nancy suggested casually.

"Maybe." Lindsay looked doubtful. "Well,
I'd better get my errands done. I want to get
home and put in a practice run before it gets
dark."

"Okay. Thanks for taking me crafts shopping. I'll see you soon," Nancy said. She waved
and headed down the street.

As soon as Nancy had turned a corner and
was out of Lindsay's sight, she ducked into a
large office building. She had to find a pay
phone.

Nancy dialed the number of the Wilcox house and asked for her father. A moment later he came on the line.

"Hi, Dad," she said. "I'm still downtown. Things are taking a little longer than I thought." She didn't tell her father about being pushed down the stairs—it would only upset him. "Do you know where Mr. Wilcox is? I need to talk to him."

"Funny you should ask," Nancy's father replied grimly. "I just got off the phone with him. The police asked him to come in for questioning, and it looks like he'll be there all day. He asked me to join him."

Nancy's heart sank. Did this mean the police had new evidence? "I'll meet you there, if that's okay," she told her father. She got directions to the police headquarters, then said goodbye.

Since Carson would not reach the city for some time, Nancy retraced her steps and entered the jewelry store she'd seen Amanda leave. If she was lucky, she could resolve two issues while she was there.

She looked around the store. As she had guessed from its fancy sign and display windows, it was an exclusive shop. The pieces of jewelry shown in the glass cases were obviously very expensive.

"A friend suggested I come here," Nancy told the manager, who introduced himself as Mr. Feder. "Her name is Amanda Spear."

Mr. Feder nodded. "Ah yes, Miss Spear. She was here earlier this morning."

Good. Now Nancy had confirmation that Amanda had indeed been in the expensive shop.

She reached into her shoulder bag and pulled out the ivory bear. "I just bought this, and I wondered if you could check it for me. I want to be sure it's genuine walrus ivory."

Mr. Feder fitted his jeweler's glass to his eye and looked carefully at the small figurine. He turned it over, gazed at the Alaskan map and frowned. Then he laid the ivory on the counter and looked at Nancy.

"I don't understand it," he said. "The seal should be used only on Alaskan products, but this is clearly an import."

"How can you tell?" Nancy asked.

Mr. Feder picked up the bear again. "Do you see these wavy, pinkish lines in the ivory? That tells us it's from an elephant, not a walrus. We don't use anything but walrus ivory in Alaska. In fact, it's illegal to import the other kind. Young lady, this bear is contraband!"

Nancy thanked Mr. Feder, then hurried back across the street to the Totem Pole. The woman who had sold her the ivory bear had gone to lunch, so Nancy talked to the manager.

"I just bought this for a friend," she explained, holding out the bear. "I wanted to ask something about how it was made. Did you buy it directly from the artist?"

The woman shook her head. "We used to, but now our business has grown, so we have a supplier. A middleman, you might say. So far, he's been able to get us everything we want."

"Can you tell me the name of your supplier?"

"Sure." The manager flipped open a file of business cards and pulled one out. Nancy noted the name and address, then thanked the woman for her help.

As she walked back into the frigid Alaskan air, Nancy was thoughtful. The manager of the Totem Pole hadn't seemed to know her supplier was providing illegal ivory. The Totem Pole was probably an innocent victim of the smugglers.

Nancy found another pay phone and dialed the number of the Wilcox Shipping offices. She asked for Amanda.

"Amanda is out for the afternoon," the receptionist said blandly. Nancy raised her eyebrows. It seemed Amanda was lying low.

Nancy flipped open the telephone book and found Amanda's home phone number. She dialed and let it ring, but there was no answer.

It was time to meet her father at the police

station. Since the address she had been given was only a few blocks from the Totem Pole, Nancy walked there. She found her father and Henry Wilcox waiting in a small conference room.

"Detective Chandler is taking a phone call. He'll be here in a minute. What have you found out?" Henry asked eagerly.

"I think the ivory is being loaded onto your ships in Seattle," Nancy told him, explaining that both the beans and the cookies had been loaded there. "The only other cargo that came from Seattle was a bunch of paperback books. I'd like to check them before they're unloaded."

Henry shook his head. "You're too late. The police let us unload the ship this morning."

Undaunted, Nancy pulled her pad from her shoulder bag. "I've got the names of the stores where the cartons are going. Maybe we can check there. And I've also found out that some of the ivory carvings sold in the Totem Pole are illegal."

"Great," Carson said. "We can tell Chandler about it when he returns."

"Your father said you wanted to ask me some questions," Henry told Nancy. "You know I'll do whatever I can to help." He heaved a gloomy sigh.

Nancy's blue eyes were bright with compassion. "I know you will. First of all, I wondered whether you had told any of your employees about the smuggling charges." She didn't think he had, but she knew she should confirm this before she tracked Amanda down for questioning.

"As we agreed, I didn't mention it to anyone," Henry said, frowning.

As she had thought. "I also wondered about John Tilden's background," Nancy said carefully.

"John?" Henry sounded surprised. "Surely you don't suspect him."

Nancy shrugged her shoulders. "At this point, I don't know," she said honestly. "I need some more information about him, such as where he worked before he came to you."

"Before he came to Anchorage, he worked as a butler for a railroad executive in Seward."

"Was he there a long time?" Nancy asked.

"No," Henry admitted. "He told me he was let go after two days. I didn't press him as to the reason for the firing."

Carson looked at Henry. "Why did you hire him?"

Henry shrugged. "My instincts told me he was a good man, and so far they've been right. John has been an excellent butler—and I like him."

"One more question," Nancy said. "I saw

from the employment records that Steve used to work for you. I wondered why he quit."

A frown crossed Henry's face. "If you want to know that, you'll have to ask Steve. I assure you, though, it has nothing to do with this case."

Nancy was about to press him further when the door to the conference room opened and Detective Chandler strode in. He grunted when he saw Nancy.

"I'm afraid I'll have to ask you to leave," he told her. "This is official business—only the suspect and his counsel have the right to be here."

Chandler's tone was firm. Nancy thought of pointing out that Carson wasn't Henry's counsel, but she knew that wouldn't help Henry any. Swallowing her disappointment, she said goodbye and headed back to the Wilcox mansion.

Nancy was deeply preoccupied during the entire drive back. The miles flew by unnoticed. When she arrived at the Wilcox mansion, she was greeted by an ecstatic George.

"I had the most fabulous day!" George exclaimed. "Steve and I spent the whole day working with the dogs."

"That's great," Nancy said.

"We took them out for a long run, and then we made them this really disgusting goop for lunch." George wrinkled her nose playfully, then babbled on. "Steve really loves his team —he'd spend all day just mucking around in the barn with them if he could, only he says Craig always beats him to the chores these days. He's going to help Craig buy his own team—that's going to be his Christmas present. Don't tell Craig, okay?"

"Mmm, that's terrific," Nancy said absently.

George gave her a long look. "You don't sound very excited," she commented. "Were you even listening to me?"

"Sorry," Nancy said contritely. "It's just that my day's been pretty rough. Don't tell Dad, but I took a tumble down a flight of stairs, thanks to someone's helping hand."

"Someone pushed you?" George exclaimed, her dark eyes widening. "Who do you think it was?"

"I'm not sure. By the time I landed, whoever it was had disappeared. I went back to the shipping offices, though, and Craig and John were there."

"Do you think it was one of them?"

Nancy shrugged. "At this point, all I know is that they were there. One of them could have pushed me. But so could Amanda Spear."

"Amanda?" This time George really was surprised. "You suspect Amanda?"

Nancy gave a tired chuckle. "I can see we've got some catching up to do," she said. "Let's go up to our room—I need to lie down and rest my aching bones for a few minutes. While I'm doing that, I'll tell you all about *my* day."

That night it snowed heavily, and a few lazy flakes were still falling when the girls came down for breakfast the next morning. Both Steve and Craig were keyed up during the meal. It was the day of the first trial run.

"We're in luck," Craig said. "Steve's dogs run well in deep snow. Some of the other teams don't."

Nancy and George offered to help the boys get the team ready, but they refused.

"They get excited when there are strangers around, and we want to store up all their enthusiasm for the race," Steve said.

Several hours later Nancy and George drove to the state park where the trials were taking place. Once they turned off the main road, they had no trouble finding the spot. The parking lot was filled with trucks carrying wooden doghouses, and the sound of excited yipping filled the air.

Craig and Steve were harnessing the last of the team when Nancy and George arrived.

"I'm glad you're here to see me win," Steve said, smiling at George.

Lindsay's team was right near Steve's, and

she must have overheard his words. "Pretty confident, aren't you?" she called over.

Steve grinned. "Just realistic. I've been working hard. Today I'm going to prove I'm a better musher than you."

Lindsay raised a skeptical eyebrow and turned away.

A crowd was beginning to gather, and Nancy scanned the spectators, searching for Amanda. Though it was a work day, the trials had been arranged so that people could come on their lunch break. But there was no sign of the bookkeeper.

Craig gave Thunder a gentle pat on his nose, then turned to Nancy. "Is your father coming?"

Nancy thought it was better not to mention that her father and Henry were at the police station. It might upset Steve and weaken his concentration. "I don't think so," she replied. "He and Mr. Wilcox are at the office today."

Steve glowered at Craig. "You can bet your life Dad won't come!" he said bitterly.

Once again, the depth of Steve's hostility toward his father surprised Nancy. She was dying to ask about it, but she held back. Just before Steve's key trial was not the right time.

"Where's the best view?" she asked. "George and I want to be sure we see everything."

Steve pointed to the opposite side of the

field. "If you stand over there, you can see the last turn and the finish line. That's usually the most exciting place to be."

Craig nodded. "As soon as Steve takes off, I'll join you there."

It was almost noon, and the teams were starting to pull into position, two to a row. As the two teams with the best cumulative scores of the season, Steve and Lindsay were in front, side by side.

Steve flashed a smile at George, then bent down and spoke to his team. An instant later, the starting bell sounded.

The teams were off!

The course was a mile long, and when the trail wound into the forest, Nancy and George could no longer see the teams. There was, however, no doubt that the race was on. The sound of the dogs' excited cries echoed through the trees.

When the teams appeared a few minutes later, Steve and Lindsay were still even. Their lead dogs were in a dead heat. It looked as if Lindsay wasn't going to let Steve win without a fight.

Nancy watched the teams round the corner, then glanced at the crowd of spectators on the opposite side. Craig was still over there, talking to a man in a big fur hat.

Then Nancy noticed John Tilden standing

only a few feet away. It seemed odd that John was there. He hadn't struck her as a sled-dog enthusiast.

When the first team emerged from the forest on the second lap, it was Steve's, clearly in the lead. A second later Lindsay appeared, but the distance between Steve's team and hers was growing.

Soon Nancy forgot everything except the excitement of the race. Steve headed into the forest on the third lap, his lead undeniable. Then somehow Lindsay caught up to him, for both teams came out into the open together. Once again the dogs were running side by side. They stayed side by side for the fourth lap.

"I can't believe it!" George cried. "It's going to be a photo finish."

"There's one more lap," Nancy said.

"Steve's going to win. He's got to." George clapped her hands together excitedly.

This time when the dogs burst out of the forest, Lindsay's team was ahead by a few feet. If Steve was going to win, he'd have to coax a last burst of speed from his dogs.

As Lindsay's team hurtled ahead, a loud crack echoed through the crisp winter air. for a brief instant no one reacted. Then Lindsay's team swerved from the trail. The young woman tugged desperately on the lines, shouting to her dogs to get them back on the track.

But the dogs were out of control, and the sled was headed straight for Nancy and George!

Chapter

Ten

Nancy moved instinctively, shoving George to the ground and flinging herself down next to her. She heard the dogs' labored breathing and the jingle of their harness as they raced past, snow spraying up from their paws. The sled's runners hissed by, only inches from her head. Then it was over, as suddenly as it had begun.

"What happened?" George asked shakily, climbing to her feet and brushing snow from her pants.

Nancy stood slowly. "Something spooked Lindsay's team."

She turned. Lindsay had her dogs under control and was headed back toward them.

She stopped the team and set the brake on the sled.

"Are you all right?" she asked anxiously.

"We're fine," George said, somewhat abruptly.

Lindsay's relief was obvious. "I'm so sorry. I don't know what happened back there. All I could think about when Butterscotch swerved was that you might be hurt."

Nancy managed a laugh. "I never thought I'd see the end of the race from quite that angle." She shaded her eyes with her hand and gazed at the finish line. Steve had apparently crossed it first. Now she could see him running back toward the scene of the accident.

Moments later he and Craig reached the girls. "Are you okay? What happened?" Steve demanded. He put a protective arm around George.

Lindsay's face was still pale as she spoke. "It sounded as if someone cracked a whip near my team. Butterscotch went wild, the way she always does when she hears a whip."

Steve gave Lindsay an irritated look. "You pamper those dogs too much. They ought to be used to loud noises."

"That's not the point," Craig said, putting a cautionary hand on his friend's arm.

Nancy looked dubious. "I don't think it was a whip, Lindsay." She turned to George. "Did you see anyone crack a whip?"

"No," said George.

"I didn't either," Nancy told them.

"I don't know what it was then," Lindsay said, with a glance at Steve. "Obviously, though, someone didn't want me to win the trial."

Steve flushed. "You can't think I had anything to do with it."

"Can't I?" Lindsay glared. "You said you were going to win, one way or another."

But Nancy wasn't listening to the conversation anymore. She'd just spotted John Tilden walking away from the track toward the parking lot. She turned to George. "Would you wait here?" she asked softly so that the others would not overhear her. "I want to talk to John."

George nodded, and Nancy walked quickly across the field.

"John!" she called.

He looked back, then stopped when he saw her.

"I want to talk to you," she said when she reached him.

"What about?" he asked warily.

"Did you have anything to do with spooking those dogs?" Nancy asked in a matter-of-fact tone.

John's mouth dropped open. "No!" he cried. His shock seemed genuine. "I heard the shot, but I don't know where it came from."

91

"The shot?" Nancy repeated. "Lindsay thought someone cracked a whip."

"It sounded like a shot to me," John said.

"What *are* you doing here, John?" Nancy asked. "I didn't know you were interested in dogsledding."

"I like Steve," he said with a touch of defiance. "I wanted to see him win."

Despite his answer, something was making John nervous. Nancy decided to try direct confrontation. "What are you hiding?" she demanded.

John stared at her, and she could see him wavering. Then his eyes dropped to the ground. "Nothing," he insisted in a low voice.

"I don't believe you," Nancy said bluntly. "You've been acting like a man with a secret. First you acted really strangely in the phone closet, even though no one could hear a word you were saying. Then you tried to hide the letter someone delivered to you. And what about when you spilled that hot cherry liqueur on me? Was that really an accident?"

John gaped at her. "Of course it was! Look, I was nervous," he admitted. "That was the first time I heard that you were a detective, and it rattled me."

"Why?" Nancy asked.

At first John didn't answer. Then he said slowly, "I thought you might be investigating me. I was afraid of losing my job."

"Like you did the last one?" Nancy said softly.

John's face whitened. "How'd you find out about that?"

"I'm a detective, remember." Nancy took a step closer to John. "I wasn't investigating you. But I think you'd be much better off if you told me the whole story now."

John bowed his head. His whole body seemed to sag as he began speaking.

"I have a kid brother who got involved with a rough crowd in Fairbanks," he said. "That's where we used to live. Jim started gambling, lost a lot of money, and—well, it's a long story, but he got desperate. There's no excuse, and I know it, but . . ." John paused and kicked at the snow.

"But?" Nancy prompted gently.

John took a deep breath. "He—he stole some money from his boss. Of course he got caught and went to prison, and there was some publicity. I couldn't stand it, so I left Fairbanks and went to Seward. I thought I'd start a new life, only it didn't work out that way. I got a job, but when they checked into my past they found out about Jim." He lifted his hands in a sad gesture. "So they fired me. Told me not to ask for references."

"That's not fair," Nancy said indignantly. "You shouldn't be punished for your brother's crime."

"You're telling me!" John's voice was bitter. "But what could I do? I tried getting a job at a few other places in Seward, but no one would hire me—I guess the word had spread."

"So you came to Anchorage," Nancy guessed.

"So I came to Anchorage," he confirmed. "I was careful this time, and I didn't tell Mr. Wilcox about my brother. I warned Jim to send his letters to a friend so Mr. Wilcox would never see the prison return address. And when I call my brother, I try not to let anyone know about it."

"You shouldn't have worried," Nancy began, but John wasn't listening to her.

"Then you came," he said, and frowned. "When I heard you were a detective, I thought Mr. Wilcox had hired you to check on my background. I panicked."

Nancy nodded. "I believe you," she said, "but I think you'd better tell Mr. Wilcox the truth."

"I guess I have to," John reluctantly agreed. They headed for the parking lot. Steve and Craig were loading the last of the dogs onto the truck. The sled was waiting to be strapped on top.

"Hi, everybody," Nancy called. Her grin faded at the sight of George's face. Though her friend tried to smile, she couldn't hide the distress in her eyes.

"Is something wrong?" Nancy asked quietly.

George's nod was almost imperceptible. "Later," she murmured.

The boys climbed down from the truck, and Nancy walked over to Steve, holding out her hand. "I never got to congratulate you," she said.

He took her hand and shook it. "I told you I'd win," he said with a grin. It was the first time Steve had been friendly to Nancy.

When Nancy and George got into the car, George was quiet, her expression grave.

"Oh, Nancy, I can't believe it." George's voice was low and angry.

Nancy looked at her. "What's wrong?"

George's dark eyes were sad. "Steve did it. He's the one who spooked Lindsay's team."

"What do you mean?" Nancy demanded. "How do you know he did it?"

George exhaled slowly before telling Nancy, "I found a whip hidden on his sled!"

Chapter

Eleven

A WHIP?" For a moment Nancy's heart sank. Then she realized what was wrong with George's idea. "But if Steve had used a whip, we'd have seen it. It's not something we could have missed."

George looked as though she wanted to believe Nancy, but she was still skeptical. "If he wasn't going to use it, why was it hidden on the sled?"

Nancy shrugged. "I don't know. I think we ought to ask Steve that question, don't you?"

When they reached the house, Nancy and George found Steve in the den, watching television.

"Where's Craig?" Nancy asked.

"He's putting the dogs back in the barn, and

then he's going to sleep." Steve's reply was curt. "Remember that he works at my esteemed father's establishment most nights," he added sarcastically.

Nancy switched off the television and turned to face Steve. Confrontation had worked with John. Maybe it would work with Steve, too.

"Did you spook Lindsay's team?" she asked bluntly.

Steve jumped to his feet. "What? No way!" he cried.

"Why did you have a whip on your sled if you didn't plan to use it?" George asked quietly.

Steve whirled around. "What are you talking about?" he demanded. "What whip?"

"You didn't hide it very well, Steve." George's look was anguished. "I found it in the sled basket, close enough to the handlebar that you could have reached it without any trouble."

For a second Steve was silent, a muscle in his jaw flexing. Finally he spoke. "Let me say three things. Number one, I didn't hide any whip. Two, I didn't reach for any whip. Three, I didn't *use* any whip. That's all there is to it."

"Steve, it's not that simple," Nancy answered. "When you got to the last lap, Lindsay was ahead. Her team would have won—except that the dogs were driven off the track by the sound of a cracking whip. We all heard it. Now, you told everyone you were going to win the trial. Also, you know that her team goes wild at the sound of a whip. *And* a whip was found on your sled. You've got to admit, there's a pretty strong case against you."

"Very nice logic, Miss Detective," Steve snapped. "You've got it all figured out, haven't you? But you're wrong. I had nothing to do with it. And I don't need to prove myself to you."

"I—I believe you, Steve," George spoke up, and laid a gentle hand on his shoulder. "But do you have any idea how that whip got onto your sled?"

Steve shrugged. "I don't know. I haven't used a whip at all this season. Lindsay gave me a hard time about it all last year, and then Amanda started in, too. I finally gave up and told Craig to throw the thing away. It wasn't worth all the grief."

"There's something else I want to ask you," Nancy said to Steve.

"Should I call my attorney?" he demanded sarcastically. "After that last question, you'll probably accuse me of being the smuggler."

George gasped. "You don't believe that, do you, Nancy?"

Now Nancy knew she was treading on very delicate ground. Instead of answering the question directly, she turned to Steve. "I'd like to know why you quit your job at Wilcox Shipping."

Steve's face darkened with anger. "Why don't you ask my father?"

"He told me to ask you," she responded evenly.

Steve spun around and stared into the fireplace. "It's no secret that my father and I don't agree on a lot of things," he said over his shoulder. "He wants me to carry on the family business. He doesn't care that I'm not interested in the shipping industry. I want to race dogs professionally. But to him, they're only a hobby."

"I'm sure he cares. It's just that—" George began, but Nancy hushed her. She wanted to hear Steve's side of the story.

"For a while we worked out a compromise," Steve went on. "Dad hired Craig to help with the dogs, and I took a job at the company." Nancy saw his fists clench. "I tried," he said in a tight voice. "I really did, but I hated it. I'm just not cut out to work in an office."

"Many people aren't," Nancy commented.

"Dad didn't see it that way," Steve said bitterly.

George took his hand in hers. "So what happened?" she urged.

"Oh, I messed up a couple of the accounts. It was bound to happen—I just can't do that kind of stuff. Anyway, Dad and I had a big fight. I left the company. And I can tell you this, I'm never going back. I don't want anything to do with Wilcox Shipping." Defiantly, Steve concluded, "If you've got any more questions, save them, because I've had enough for today."

He walked out of the room. George bit her lip as she watched him go.

"Oh, Nancy, he's not a criminal," she burst out when the door had closed behind Steve. "He just needs someone to tell him he's not a loser. Did you have to push him so hard?"

Nancy sighed. "I needed answers, George," she said patiently. "I got some. But there are still a few questions I'd like to ask Steve." Like what he meant when he said I'd "mess up everything," she added to herself.

"He's not a criminal," George repeated. Her lips set in a stubborn line. "I know it. And I know you'll find the same thing."

"I really do hope you're right," Nancy told her friend sincerely.

George went after Steve to see if she could talk to him. Nancy walked to the telephone closet. She still had to find Amanda.

After calling the shipping company's offices, Nancy found out that Amanda Spear had called in sick. There was no answer at her apartment, however. Then Nancy phoned Lindsay.

"No, I haven't seen Amanda since right before the trials," Lindsay said.

"Before the trials? You mean she was there?" Nancy asked, surprised. "I didn't see her."

"Well, she was at the starting line, but she must have left pretty quickly. I looked for her afterward, but I couldn't find her," Lindsay said. "She sure has been acting weird lately."

"Thanks, Lindsay. Listen, I've got to go," Nancy said. She hung up and came out of the phone closet. So Amanda had been at the trials. What significance did that fact have?

Nancy's head was beginning to ache. She took a deep breath and stretched. The movement made all her bruises ache again and reminded her of what she'd been through in the last two days.

Maybe I'll just lie down on the couch in the den and think for a little while, she decided. There's not much I can do until Dad and Mr. Wilcox get back, anyway. And I'm so tired!

Going into the den, she closed the door quietly behind her and stretched out on the couch. I'll just shut my eyes for a minute, she told herself. Just for a minute . . .

Nancy woke with a start at the sound of a door slamming. Then she heard the voices of her father and Henry Wilcox. Peering groggily at her watch, she realized that it was almost six o'clock. She had slept the afternoon away! Shaking her head, she went upstairs to wash her face before dinner.

At dinner Nancy learned only that the interview with Detective Chandler hadn't had any results one way or the other. Carson Drew and Henry Wilcox weren't saying more—they made a determined effort to keep the conversation light.

Carson regaled Nancy and George with tales of his day. "Now I know how the other half lives," he said, grinning at Henry. "My friend here told me he had business in Juneau, so we took his company plane, and off we went to the capital for the afternoon. Tomorrow we're going to Fairbanks."

Henry laughed. "It isn't that unusual to have a private plane in Alaska. We have so few roads here that planes are sometimes the only means of transportation."

"Almost as good as dog sleds," Steve said. Nancy suspected he was trying to needle his father.

Carson turned to him. "How'd you do in the trials today?" he asked.

"I won," Steve said flatly.

Carson reached over and shook his hand. "Congratulations. I'm glad to hear that."

"So am I! Are you happy now?" Henry asked Steve.

The question hadn't sounded provocative to Nancy, but Steve gave his father an irritated look. "Not until I win the Solstice Derby. You know that."

Henry changed the subject. "We have another ship arriving tonight," he told Nancy. "The *Dall Sheep*. It'll be unloading tomorrow."

"Would you mind if I had a look around it before it unloads?" she asked.

"Not at all. In fact, I'm going to the shipyard tomorrow morning. Why don't you ride in with me?" Henry offered. "But we have to go early so that I can get back in time to fly to Fairbanks before noon."

"No problem." Nancy looked at George. "Want to come along?"

George groaned. "No thanks. I'd rather sleep."

When dinner was over, Nancy returned to the telephone closet and tried calling Amanda again. There was still no answer. One way or another, she'd have to find the girl the next day. Time was running out for Henry.

When Nancy hung up and stepped into the hallway, she found John waiting for her. "Can I talk to you?" he asked.

"Sure." Curious, Nancy followed him into the kitchen. He pulled out a chair for her and reached into his pocket.

"Here." He handed her a piece of twisted red paper.

Nancy stared at it. "What is it?" she asked. The paper looked ordinary, except for a black mark on one edge.

"I think it's what frightened Lindsay's dogs," John said. "After I left you, I started thinking about what could have made the noise. I went back and looked around. This was lying on the track." He pointed at the paper. "I was lucky that it wasn't a white one. I'd never have found it in all the snow."

"Found what?" Nancy asked, mystified. "What are you talking about?"

"It's like a firecracker. There's a mild explosive inside it, and when you hit it against something hard, it makes a loud bang." John grinned. "My brother Jim and I used to play with them. I didn't know kids still used them."

Nancy held the red paper up and examined it. Now she knew why no one had seen a whip. Any one of the spectators—including Amanda, John, and Craig—could have carried the firecracker. It was small and easy enough to use that even Steve could have done it on his sled.

Which, she thought, puts me right back where I started. Anyone could have done it— Steve or Craig to ruin Lindsay's race, Amanda —or any of them, really—to put me out of commission. The question is, *who* did do it?

As Henry Wilcox drove Nancy into Anchorage the next morning, he asked her what she was looking for on the ship that had just arrived.

"I want to see if any of the cargo was loaded in Seattle," she told him. "That's where the other smuggled shipments came from, remember?"

The *Dall Sheep* wasn't as modern as the *Musk Ox,* but it had the same air of prosperity and fresh paint that Nancy had seen on the other ship.

Henry led Nancy to the front of the ship and pulled out the cargo lists for her. "I'll leave you to look through them," he said. "I want to talk to the guard."

She searched each of the shipping receipts, looking for any cargo that had originated in Seattle, but there was none.

"Any luck?" Henry asked when he returned.

"Not much," Nancy said. "Could we stop by police headquarters? I'd like to see whether they've checked the pallets of books."

Henry agreed, but unfortunately Detective Chandler had nothing to report. They'd searched each carton, and they were all the same—filled with paperback books.

"We've had the Totem Pole's ivory supplier in for questioning, too," Detective Chandler told Nancy and Henry. "It looks as if he was duped just like everyone else."

"Who did he buy the statues from?" Nancy asked. "Did he say?"

The detective glanced quickly at his notes.

"Well, he buys a lot of his stuff from a lot of different people, and he wasn't sure which one sold him the ivory bear." Chandler looked up, and his eyes met Nancy's. "But he thinks he bought the fake at an auction outside Anchorage, from a tall young man who arrived on a dogsled."

Chapter
Twelve

A TALL YOUNG MAN on a dogsled," Nancy repeated faintly. The description fit Steve Wilcox pretty well. She glanced at Henry out of the corner of her eye, but he didn't seem to have caught the significance of Chandler's statement. Probably it had never even occurred to him to suspect his own son, Nancy realized.

Well, there was no concrete proof yet. And after all, it was possible that the supplier had met with some other tall young dogsled driver. For Henry's and George's sakes, she hoped it was so.

"Thanks, Detective Chandler," she said. Turning to Henry, she forced a cheerful smile. "Ready to head home?"

When they arrived back at the house, Henry left the car running while he went in to get Carson. Nancy followed him in.

John Tilden came in from the kitchen. "Is George up yet?" Nancy asked him. She wanted to prepare her friend for the possibility that Steve was involved in the smuggling after all.

"I saw her go outside just after you left this morning," the butler replied. "She said she was going to the kennels to look for Steve."

Nancy headed back outside. As she approached the barn, the dogs' excited barking told her someone was inside with them.

Nancy slid the wooden door open and stepped inside, blinking as her eyes adjusted from bright light to the dim interior. Steve was standing near the barrel stove in the middle of the floor, stirring a large pot of a strong-smelling substance. Craig was at the far end of the building, once again cleaning straw out of the dogs' beds.

"Hi!" she called. "Have you seen George?"

Steve turned toward Nancy, still holding the wooden spoon in his hand. "I thought she went into Anchorage with you and Dad."

Nancy shook her head. "John said she came out here early this morning." She walked closer to see what Steve was stirring. "What is that?" she asked, wrinkling her nose.

"Dog food. Want a taste?" Steve dipped the

spoon back into the thick mixture and drew out a sample. "Fish, beaver, lamb, and liver—nothing but the finest ingredients for my dogs."

Nancy grimaced. "It sounds awful, and it smells even worse."

Steve gave her a tolerant smile. "The dogs need the nutrients. They race better when they've eaten a meal like this." He put the spoon back into the pot, then called to Craig, "Do you know where George is?"

Craig dropped the shovel into a pile of straw and walked toward them. "George?" he repeated. "She was here first thing this morning. She said she was going to Lindsay's." He looked at his watch. "That was a couple of hours ago, though. She ought to be back by now."

Nancy was surprised. George hadn't mentioned that plan to her. She thanked Craig for the information, then headed back to the house. Hurrying to the telephone, she looked up Lindsay's number and dialed.

No answer. She tried again, thinking she might have misdialed. Still no answer.

Nancy wrote down Lindsay's address, grabbed the keys to the car Henry had lent her, and headed for the garage. Five minutes later she pulled into the driveway of Lindsay's house.

She walked up the front steps and knocked on the door. No one answered.

The kennels were out back, a good distance from the house. The sound of yipping told her she was headed in the right direction. When she rounded a small bend, she saw the barn. She pushed open the door and looked around.

"Hi, Lindsay," Nancy called in greeting. "Is George still here?"

Like Steve, Lindsay was stirring a pot of vile-smelling food. She looked up at Nancy, a puzzled expression on her face.

"Was George supposed to be here?" she asked.

"She's not at the Wilcoxes', and she told Craig she was coming here," Nancy said.

Lindsay shook her head. "I haven't seen her since the trial run yesterday. I was planning to come over and see you two today, to make sure you were both okay after that fall. But with a storm coming, I had to get the dogs fed."

Lindsay gestured at the mixture she was stirring. "This is one bad thing about winter. In summer we give the dogs dry food, but they burn so many more calories in winter that we have to cook this stew. They love it, but I sure don't." Lindsay stirred the pot once more. "I wish I could feed my team pellets all year."

Nancy tried not to be impatient, though she was really beginning to wonder about George. "I was hoping George would be here," she admitted. "I thought she might have asked you for another chance to drive a dogsled."

Lindsay gave Nancy a quick glance. "If she shows up, I'll tell her to call you."

"Thanks."

Lindsay walked to the door with Nancy, then looked up at the sky. Though it had been blue an hour before, it was now gray, and there was a heaviness to the air.

"The weatherman predicted a big storm," Lindsay remarked. "Looks like it's going to happen."

As Nancy slid behind the steering wheel, she frowned. It wasn't like George to disappear without telling anyone. What if she was in trouble? She could have gone for a walk and gotten lost in the woods, or something. Maybe Nancy should raise an alarm.

She was about to start her car when she saw a battered old sedan pulling into Lindsay's driveway. The driver's door opened, and Amanda Spear got out.

"Amanda," Nancy whispered. She couldn't pass up this chance to talk to her most elusive suspect. Jumping out of her car, she hurried over to block Amanda's path. "Hello," she said cheerfully. "I've been looking for you. I missed you at the trials yesterday."

Whatever reaction Nancy had expected, it wasn't the one she got. Amanda's face turned an angry shade of red. "If you want to gloat over Steve's victory, don't bother," she snapped. "He may have beaten Lindsay, but it wasn't a fair race." Her voice was filled with scorn. "Steve's got every advantage. His father gives him all the money he needs, and he's got a trainer who can take the dogs out every morning."

Nancy started to interrupt, but the other girl wouldn't let her speak.

"Don't try to deny it. I saw those dogs on my way to work this morning. I tell you, Nancy, it makes me sick. Steve's a spoiled brat."

Nancy held up a hand to stop Amanda's tirade. "I don't want to talk about Steve's dog team."

Amanda's expression changed. "Oh?" she said cautiously.

"Look, why don't we go sit in my car?" Nancy suggested. "It's freezing out here."

"Why?" Amanda asked. "How long is this going to take?"

Nancy looked at her levelly. "That's up to you," she said.

Amanda stared at Nancy for a long minute. Then she turned toward the car. "Let's go."

The girls got into the car, and Nancy turned on the ignition so that she could run the heater. Amanda, seated in the passenger seat, folded her hands in her lap. "What do you want?" she asked.

"I want some real answers from you."

Amanda twisted a lock of hair around one finger. "What are you talking about?" she said, and Nancy noted the quaver in her voice.

"What do you know about the ivory that's been smuggled on the Wilcox ships?" she demanded.

Amanda's eyes flew wide open. She looked utterly dumbfounded. "What ivory?"

"You know—the little carved puffins and bears. Was it Steve's idea?" Nancy asked. That was a shot in the dark, but she had to start this conversation somewhere. "Is that how you got involved?"

Amanda's face was white. "I don't know anything about any smuggling. How could I be involved in something I know nothing about?"

Nancy looked at her for a long moment. "You have a motive and opportunity, and you've certainly been acting very strangely."

Amanda reacted instantly. "Wait a minute! You'd better explain all that."

"Let's start with opportunity," Nancy said. "You work at Wilcox, so you have access to the shipping schedules and practically every piece of information about the company. It wouldn't be hard to arrange an illegal shipment of ivory."

"A lot of people have access to that same information," Amanda said hotly. "Everyone from the receptionist to the night watchman knows the schedule."

"That may be true," Nancy agreed, "but how many people have acted the way you did? You disappeared right after I was pushed down the stairs, and—"

Amanda interrupted. "What are you talking about? When were you pushed down the stairs?"

Nancy explained about the mysterious hand that had pushed her down the stairs.

Amanda's gray eyes flashed with concern. "You could have been badly hurt."

Nancy nodded. "I assume that was the general idea," she said dryly.

"It wasn't me," Amanda cried. "Whatever you think about me, I would never, ever do that."

Nancy watched Amanda closely, trying to decide if she was telling the truth or if she was an accomplished actress.

"You said I had a motive for smuggling," Amanda continued. "What do you mean by that?"

"Money. Amanda, I saw your salary when I was going through the books. There's no way you can afford all those furs and that huge gold ring." Nancy's eyes dropped to Amanda's right hand. It was bare. "Where *is* your ring?"

Tears welled in Amanda's eyes. "Oh, Nancy,

I've been so *dumb,"* she said, her voice cracking. "You're right. I can't afford those furs. The payments are way over my head. I tried to return them to the store, but the furrier just laughed at me. He said no one wants used furs."

Amanda held out the hand that no longer sported the gold nugget ring. "I'd already sold Craig my share of the cabin that he and I inherited from our grandfathers. And I took a couple of advances on my paycheck—that was why I got so nervous when you wanted to see the books. It's not illegal or anything, but I should have asked Mr. Wilcox." She paused, gulping back tears.

"Go on," Nancy prodded.

"The only thing I had left of any value was my ring. I didn't have any choice. I had to sell it. I needed the money to pay for the furs." Tears began to trickle down her face. "That ring was a gift from my grandfather, too. He had it made from the first nugget he panned and gave it to me for my sixteenth birthday. Now I've lost it, all because I was so silly."

"I still don't see why you've been avoiding me," Nancy said.

Amanda turned her tearstained face toward Nancy. "The day you came to look at the books was the day I had to see the jeweler. I was nervous because I didn't want to go. And when you asked to see the books, I got scared that you'd tell Mr. Wilcox I'd been borrowing on my salary."

Nancy nodded. So far, Amanda's story had the sound of truth.

"Later on," Amanda continued, "I saw you and Lindsay across the street and heard you calling me, but I had just sold the ring, and I was so upset I didn't want to talk to anyone. That's why I walked the other way and went into the lobby of that building. There was a bunch of people going in, so I got into the middle of the group to avoid the doorman and went up in the elevator." She looked at Nancy again. "I waited there until I thought you'd probably given up looking for me. Then I went home."

"I tried to call you at home," Nancy told her.

Amanda shrugged. "I heard the phone, but I didn't feel like talking to anyone." She looked at her hand again. "To someone else it may have been just a ring, but it was my last link to my grandfather. The furs aren't worth losing that. I've been an idiot."

Nancy touched Amanda's shoulder to comfort her. She felt a sense of relief after hearing her story. Amanda wasn't involved in the smuggling. She was a girl who'd made a foolish mistake and was now paying for it.

Amanda pulled out a tissue and blew her nose. "What did you mean about Steve?" she asked in a muffled voice. "You know, when you asked if I'd gotten involved through him. You don't think he'd use his own father as a cover for criminal activities, do you? Because I have to tell you, Steve would never do anything like that. I know I don't say many nice things about him, but he's not a criminal."

Steve's not a criminal. George had said the same thing, Nancy reflected.

George! Suddenly Nancy remembered that her friend was still unaccounted for. "I don't know anything for sure yet," she told Amanda. "But I'll find out, don't worry. I've got to get back to the Wilcoxes' now." She smiled at the other girl as Amanda got out of the car. "Thanks for being honest with me."

Nancy drove back to the Wilcox house and hurried inside. She checked the foyer closet, but George's parka was not there.

Going back outside, Nancy noticed that it had started to snow. She walked to the barn. It was silent, and when she went inside the dogs were gone. So was the sled. Steve and Craig must have taken them out for a run.

Nancy walked through the barn slowly. Something bothered her about George's disappearance, but she couldn't quite put her finger on it. She found herself standing by the stall where Steve and Craig stored the burlap bags of dry dog food.

As Nancy looked around, a tiny scrap of bright red cloth near the floor caught her eye. It had snagged on a nail that stuck halfway out of a wooden post. She bent quickly to examine it.

Nancy thought she recognized it. It looked as though it had been torn from George's silk scarf, the one that her mother had given her just before they left River Heights.

Then Nancy spotted something that sent chills rippling down her spine. Half under the pallet that the bags of dog food lay on, and almost buried by straw, was the rest of George's scarf.

Gingerly, Nancy lifted it up. It had been ripped almost in two.

Quickly she strode around the pallet to examine the rest of the stall. On the other side, the straw had been kicked away from the wood floor, and one of the bags of dog food had been ripped open. Brown, freeze-dried nuggets had spilled out over the floor. That told Nancy all she needed to know. A struggle had taken place here.

Her sharp eyes noticed something glinting inside the gaping hole in the bag of dog food. Carefully, Nancy reached inside and pushed her hand through the loose nuggets. She felt something hard and smooth and took it out. It was a small ivory carving of a bear.

Nancy's mind stood still for a second as she took in the little carving. Then it was churning again. Things were falling into place.

And then she knew, with absolute certainty, who the smuggler was.

Chapter

Thirteen

MOTIVE AND OPPORTUNITY. One person had them both.

"Craig Miller," Nancy said aloud.

His motive was simple. He'd made no secret of needing money so that he could afford his own dog team. And as the night watchman at the shipyard, he had access to the ships. He could slip into the cargo hold and unload the ivory while he was supposed to be on duty.

Craig had been at the shipyard when the lights went off in the cargo hold. He'd been at the office when Nancy was pushed down the stairs. He'd been at the track when the firecracker exploded.

Nancy thought about how Craig had said

that Steve made him do all the chores. That was a clever lie—it made Steve look like an insensitive rich kid, and it also made it seem perfectly natural that Craig never let anyone else near the food bags where his illegal ivory was cached.

Craig had had luck on his side, too, she reflected. The Totem Pole's ivory supplier had described a "tall young man driving a dogsled," and Nancy had immediately assumed it was Steve. But Craig was nearly as tall as Steve, if only she had stopped to think about it.

The clues had been there all along. But through it all, Craig had drawn Nancy's suspicions to other people—he'd suggested John was hiding something. He'd led her along a trail of lies.

Nancy was willing to bet it was Craig who'd concealed the whip on Steve's sled, and now he'd done something to George!

Nancy bit her finger as she tried to think. If I were Craig, what would I have done with someone who walked in on me and caught me red-handed? she wondered. Where would I take her where no one else would find her?

Suddenly an idea struck her. Nancy ran back to the house and raced up the porch stairs two at a time. "John!" she called, barging into the kitchen. But the butler wasn't there. To her surprise, Nancy found Steve in the kitchen, making himself a sandwich. Her heart sank. She'd thought he was with Craig.

"Where's Craig?" she asked, unable to disguise the tension in her voice.

Steve turned and looked at her as if she were slightly demented. "He went out after we trained the dogs today."

Nancy walked over and stood directly in front of Steve. There was no time for their personal disagreements. Too much hinged on taking swift action.

"Listen, Steve, and listen carefully. We don't have very much time. Did you take the dogs out for a run first thing this morning?"

Steve slapped a piece of cheese onto his sandwich. "No. Craig did. He does that every morning."

"Then you've got to help me," Nancy said.

"Is this another one of your great melodramas?" Steve asked skeptically. He picked up his plate and headed for the den.

"I'm serious!" Nancy insisted, following him.

Steve looked at her. "I hate to tell you this, but you're the last person on earth I want to help. You've caused a whole lot of trouble around here." He plopped down on the couch.

Nancy reached down and grabbed Steve's shoulder. "Forget how you feel about me," she said fiercely. "Think about George. She's in trouble."

There was a flicker of concern in Steve's eyes. "What about George?" he demanded.

"She wasn't at Lindsay's house as Craig had said," Nancy explained. She took the small ivory bear from her parka pocket and held it in front of the young man. "I found this hidden in the barn." Quickly she explained how she had seen the torn scarf, the signs of struggle—and her suspicions about Craig Miller.

"John told me George went out to the kennels early this morning looking for you. I think she accidentally caught Craig red-handed when he was hiding the carvings. So he kidnapped her. Steve, she's in terrible danger. Craig could do anything!"

Steve stood, a look of disbelief on his face. He took a menacing step toward Nancy. "I don't believe you!" he cried. "Craig's my friend. He's not a kidnapper."

Nancy stood her ground, speaking calmly but forcefully. "Steve, there's no time to waste. I know you don't like me, but we've got to work together. It's the only way we can save George."

Perhaps it was the urgency in her voice. Or perhaps Steve knew that Nancy cared for George as much as he did. Doubt flickered through his eyes. He took a deep breath.

"What is it you want me to do?" he asked, finally.

"We need to get to Craig's grandfather's cabin. I'm sure he took George there this morning when he took the dogs out. We've got to get there before he hurts her."

Steve sighed. "Well, we can take the dogs," he suggested, going out to the foyer. "But you're wrong about Craig. You'll see."

"Steve," Nancy said, "the dogs are gone."

"What?" Steve's face went slack with shock. Then he grabbed his parka and put on his boots. As soon as he was ready, he and Nancy ran to the barn. They slid the wooden door open, and Nancy watched Steve's eyes widen as he took in the rows of empty straw beds.

"Craig took them!" There was a note of surprise and horror in Steve's voice. Until this moment, Nancy could tell, he hadn't really believed her. Now he knew she was right.

Steve wasted no words. "There are no roads to the cabin," he said. "Can you ski or snow-shoe?"

Nancy shook her head. "Too slow. Let's go to Lindsay's. We'll use her team."

"Okay." Steve nodded.

The snow was falling thicker now. Nancy handed Steve the keys to the car. "You're better than I am at driving in this weather."

The roads were already treacherously icy, and the drive was a slow one. Finally they saw the welcoming lights of Lindsay's house. Nancy jumped out and raced up the stairs, pressing the doorbell and knocking on the door at the same time.

Within seconds Lindsay opened the door. "What's wrong?" she asked.

Steve was only one step behind Nancy as she entered the house.

"It's George," Nancy said. "We need your dogs to save her." Quickly she explained the situation to the astonished girl.

Lindsay sat down heavily on her couch. "I can't believe this. *Craig?*" she said faintly. Then she looked up at Nancy and Steve. "I'm sorry. Of course I'll help," she said. She reached into the closet and started throwing on her heavy clothes.

Steve shook his head. "We can't all go on the sled. It would be too much weight for the dogs."

"Steve's the only one who knows the way, Lindsay." Nancy fixed her eyes on the other girl. "Please. Let us use your team."

Lindsay hesitated. "Right!" she said at last.

They raced out to the kennels. At Lindsay's direction, Nancy unloaded the bundles from the sled and dragged it out of the barn while Lindsay and Steve harnessed the dogs.

"We'd better use booties—they'll get ice balls between their pads in this wet snow," Lindsay said when Nancy returned. "Can you get them?" She gestured to an old dresser that stood in one corner of the barn. "Third drawer."

The booties were made from a thick cotton fabric, and they had Velcro fasteners to hold them on the dogs' paws. The three put them on the dogs' feet in tense silence.

Next, Lindsay sent Nancy back to the dresser for two extra blankets. None of them knew what was in the cabin, and the extra protection from the cold might come in handy. Moments later Steve strapped Nancy into the basket of the sled and took his place on the runners.

Lindsay walked to the head of the team and whispered something in Butterscotch's ear. The lead dog gave a short bark.

In the lights from the barn, Nancy saw Lindsay smile. "You and George are in good hands," she told Nancy. "You've got a great musher."

"Thanks for the vote of confidence," Steve responded, clearly surprised by his rival's compliment. "Let's hope I earn it."

The snow was now heavier than any Nancy had ever seen. Huge flakes formed a white curtain, quickly obliterating tracks and reducing visibility to a few feet. She wondered how they'd find the trail to the cabin. To Steve's team, the route would be familiar, but Lindsay rarely took her dogs north of Anchorage.

"We'll get there," Steve told Nancy, as

though he sensed her worries. "The dogs are used to finding new trails."

The team was clearly eager to run. They barked and tugged at the line, urging Steve to give the command to start.

"Hike!" he yelled.

They were off.

The snow flew into Nancy's face as the dogs pulled the sled forward. She was glad Steve had insisted she wear a face mask. The thin silk fabric protected her from the fierce cold and the blowing snow. Steve wore a battery-powered light on a band around his forehead.

When the trail started up a hill, Steve jumped off the runners and jogged behind the sled.

"Have to save the dogs' energy," he said breathlessly to Nancy. For a few minutes, there was no sound other than the swish of the sled's runners in the snow and the dogs' panting.

A large snowshoe hare darted across the trail, and the dogs swerved, starting to follow it. "Gee!" Steve shouted, tugging on the handlebar. Butterscotch turned to look at him, then led the dogs back onto the trail.

"Lindsay was right. You're very good," Nancy told Steve. Even though it wasn't his team, he had total control over it.

Nancy heard the anger in Steve's voice when he replied, "I still can't believe Craig did this."

"Let's see what he says when we get to the cabin," Nancy suggested.

Steve was quiet for a moment. When he spoke, there was grudging admiration in his voice. "You're quite a detective."

Nancy managed a laugh. "Not really. There's one mystery I haven't been able to solve."

"What's that?"

"Why you don't like me."

The trail crossed another hill, and Steve was silent as he ran behind the sled. When he climbed back on the runners, he said to Nancy, "It wasn't anything personal."

"You could have fooled me," she replied.

Nancy could hear the pain in Steve's voice, even through the wind that rushed by her ears. "Your father's always telling Dad what a great relationship you two have," he said. "For years I've heard about the wonderful Drew family. When I quit my job at the shipping company, it got worse. It seems like I've heard about nothing the past six weeks but how great you are and what a fantastic job you've done with your life so far. Well, I'm sorry I can't be you—I'm sure my dad would like me better if I were."

Nancy shook her head ruefully. "Oh, Steve, you're so wrong about your dad. He loves you. You may not believe this," she said, "but every time my dad talks to your dad, all your dad talks about is how proud he is of you."

"I'll bet." Steve was plainly skeptical.

"It's true, Steve. It really is. And another thing—maybe he wasn't going about it in the right way, but I think, by talking about me so much, your dad was probably trying to encourage you to find the life that's right for you, whatever that may be." She laughed. "I mean, you could hardly call what I do an 'office job,' could you?"

"No, I guess you couldn't," Steve said thoughtfully. "Maybe you have a point."

Nancy craned her neck to look at him in the gathering dusk. "You know I'm right," she said, and smiled at him. After a moment he returned the grin.

The snow continued to fall, and when darkness came, Nancy wondered how Steve could find his way. It seemed as though they'd been traveling for hours, although Steve assured her it had been only a little more than one hour.

"We're almost there," he said, turning the sled sharply to the right.

Nancy squinted her eyes. It wasn't her imagination. There was something dark a few hundred yards ahead of them. The cabin! Lindsay's dogs began to bark from excitement. Then the night was filled with the sound of answering barks.

Steve pulled the sled to a stop and turned off the light on his forehead. Nancy unfastened the belt that had held her in. She jumped to her feet and ran to the cabin. She flung open the door.

At first glance the cabin seemed empty. Then Nancy saw a dark form on a low cot by one wall. Heart hammering, she ran over and bent down to see who it was.

George was lying there, eyes closed. Her face was perfectly white, and her skin was icy to the touch.

"George!" Nancy said in a low, urgent voice. She shook her friend by the shoulder. But George neither spoke nor stirred. She just lay there, still as death.

Chapter

Fourteen

NANCY'S HEART STOOD STILL. "George!" she whispered again. Peeling off her mitten, she placed gentle fingers on George's throat just below the left ear.

There was a pulse. It was slow but steady. Nancy turned to Steve. "She's okay," she said quickly, seeing the expression on his face. "You'd better look for Craig—I'll take care of George."

Steve spun on his heel and went back out into the darkness. Nancy thought quickly. Craig had probably given George some kind of sedative. She had to get her friend moving to work the drug out of her system.

"George!" she called. She slapped her friend's cheeks lightly. "It's Nancy. Wake up."

At first there was no response. Then George's eyelids flickered. Her pupils were dilated, and she didn't seem to recognize Nancy.

"George! It's Nancy."

A glimmer of recognition made its way into George's eyes. "Check the dog food," the drugged girl said. Her words were slow and deliberate, as though she had to force them out. She closed her eyes again, drifting back to sleep.

Steve strode back into the cabin and stamped the snow from his boots. "Is she okay?" he demanded fiercely.

Nancy shook her head. "It looks like Craig gave her some kind of sleeping pill. We have to get her back to your house and call the doctor. Did you find Craig?" she asked.

"No—I don't know where he is," Steve said. He looked around the room, then walked to the stove that stood in one corner. He opened the large box next to it and peered inside. "Maybe he went to get wood. There's not much in here, and I didn't see any outside." He unzipped his parka. "In this weather nobody would take a chance on running out of firewood."

"How about your dogs?" Nancy asked. "Are they all right?"

Steve nodded. "They're used to being outside, even in a storm. Craig unharnessed them, so I guess he's planning to stay here for a while."

Nancy felt a cold draft sweep along the floor. She looked up.

"You bet I plan to stay," Craig's voice boomed from the open door. He was dressed in a light blue snowsuit, and his blue eyes glittered dangerously, chilling Nancy more than the arctic wind.

Craig closed the door behind him and glanced around the room. "Quite a cozy gathering, isn't it?"

Before Nancy or Steve could reply, George opened her eyes and started to sit up. When she saw Craig, she moaned and sank back onto the cot.

"What did you do to her?" Steve demanded, a worried frown etched on his face.

"Nothing." Though it was only one word, Craig's tone indicated how unimportant George was.

Steve clenched his fists and took a step toward Craig.

"Don't," Nancy warned him in a low voice. Craig's eyes blazed with excitement, as if he was looking for an excuse to fight. That was the last thing they needed.

Steve evidently realized the same thing, for he lowered his hands to his sides.

Craig sneered. "What's the matter, big man? Didn't they teach you how to fight at those fancy schools your daddy sent you to?"

"You were really clever to arrange the smuggling," Nancy said, trying to shift Craig's attention. "I still haven't figured out how you managed all the details."

"Playing for time, huh?" Craig said with a sidelong glance at Nancy. Her stomach contracted. He wasn't going to take the bait.

Then Craig smiled and leaned back against the wall. "Well, I may as well boast a little," he said easily. "Because you kids won't be going anywhere for a long, long time.

"It was all so easy," he went on. "I was out with some friends one night when I heard this guy in Seattle was looking for a partner in the shipping business—someone who wanted to make lots of money. That was right up my alley. The guy had contacts in the Far East who made ivory statues. He needed someone in Anchorage to get the stuff off a ship and into the hands of the dealers." Craig tossed his head arrogantly. "It was Craig Miller to the rescue. All I had to do was pull a fast one on old man Wilcox. Boy, is that guy slow on the uptake!"

Steve growled low in his throat and started to move toward Craig. Nancy put a cautionary hand on his arm.

Craig looked from Nancy to Steve, then

back again. "You're a little rusty yourself, Ms. Drew," he told her. "That ivory was right under all of your noses, all the time." He crowed with laughter.

Steve could control his anger no longer. "I can't believe it!" he cried. "I thought you were my friend."

Craig's laughter stopped abruptly. His voice was little more than a snarl. "Do you think I liked being one of your employees? It was demeaning having to work as your kennel boy. But you never thought about that, did you?"

Now that Craig was talking, there was no stopping him. "Do you think I liked training your dogs but never getting to race them?" he demanded. "All the work but none of the fun? I'll bet you never thought about that, any more than you thought about what it's like to be poor. Well, I'll tell you and Ms. Drew here one thing. I'm never going to be poor again."

Craig smiled, but his smile was filled with malevolence. Nancy could hardly believe this was the man who'd once been friendly to her.

"You were too smart for your own good," he told her. "You wouldn't take my hints and stop the investigation."

"Hints? You mean all those . . . mishaps?" Nancy asked carefully. Her eyes darted around the room as she sought a weapon of some kind.

"Mishaps." Craig chuckled mirthlessly. "Oh, that's very funny. Mishaps. Yes, I guess you could call tumbling down a flight of stairs and nearly being trampled by a team of runaway sled dogs 'mishaps.' "

He looked down at George, and his smile was not a pleasant thing to see. "I would have pulled it off without a hitch, you know. It was just bad luck that your pal George came in at the wrong time and saw me hiding the ivory." He pursed his lips primly. "There's a lesson in this somewhere—something about minding your own business. Too bad you all won't live to put it into practice."

That was more than Steve could take. He lunged forward to tackle the friend who'd betrayed his trust.

But Craig was quick. In one fluid motion he stepped to the side. He grabbed Steve's arm and twisted it behind his back. Then he pulled a big, old-fashioned revolver from the pocket of his parka. He raised the butt and brought it down on Steve's head.

Steve crumpled to the floor.

Nancy started toward him, but Craig's barked command stopped her. She turned and looked at him.

His eyes were serious at last. "I'm afraid this is goodbye," he said. Slowly and deliberately he raised the gun and pointed the barrel at her. "It's your turn now, Nancy Drew."

Chapter

Fifteen

Not if I can help it!" Nancy cried. Moving with reflexes that had been honed by her martial arts classes, she lunged forward and kicked up and out, catching Craig's arm.

The gun flew from his hand and landed with a loud clatter on the other side of the cabin.

"You—!" Craig's face contorted with fury. His hands reached for Nancy, the fingers curled as if to strangle her.

Nancy moved deftly to the side. Suddenly Craig lost his balance and toppled to the floor. His head hit the hard boards with a crack, and he lay still.

For the briefest instant Nancy stared at her assailant, wondering how he'd tripped. Then she saw Steve's leg where Craig had been standing. Still on the floor, Steve was conscious. He peered up at her, rubbing his head.

"Did I get him? *All right!* Let's get him tied up," he said, rising to his feet.

While Steve held Craig on the floor, Nancy found nylon twine in a cupboard. In minutes they had bound the unconscious Craig's hands and ankles. Once Nancy thought she saw his eyelids flicker. She leaned forward and peered intently at his face, but it remained slack.

"That must have been some blow to his head," she commented.

"I hope it hurt," Steve said angrily. "Come on, let's get George out of here."

The two of them bundled George into the extra blankets Nancy had brought and carried her to the sled.

Nancy was surprised at how much snow had fallen while they were in the cabin. And it kept coming down, thicker and faster.

When Steve had fastened the belt around George and was sure she was secure, he turned to Nancy.

"Here's the headlight," he said, holding out the bright battery-powered light. "Do you know how to work it?"

Nancy nodded, but there was a question in her eyes. "Why do I need it?" she asked.

"Because you're going to take George back to the house," Steve answered.

Nancy looked at him, startled by his reply. "I can't. I'm not a musher," she protested.

Steve gave her a little smile. "Let's not argue again. Someone's got to deal with Craig, and it ought to be me. He was my friend. If it hadn't been for me, you and George wouldn't have been involved in this mess." He handed Nancy the light and helped her secure it to her cap. "Get George to the doctor. I'll harness my dogs and then bring Craig back with me."

Nancy hesitated. It was fine to tell her to take the dogsled, but she was a rookie musher.

"Look, Nancy," Steve said. "This storm isn't letting up any. You'd better get going. The dogs will follow their own trail and lead you back."

"I hope you're right," Nancy told him. "And, Steve—good luck to you."

She took her place on the runners. Her right foot reached to release the brake.

"Hike!" she called.

Butterscotch turned and looked at Nancy, as though surprised by a new driver. Then she barked to the team, and the sled began to move.

"Home, Butterscotch," Nancy urged the powerful husky. "Take us home."

As the trail began to climb a hill, she jumped off the runners and ran behind the sled. Steve had made it look easy when he'd done it. After she'd crested her first hill, though, Nancy had a new respect for Steve, Lindsay, and all the other dog mushers. It was hard work running through the deep snow.

Nancy shouted words of encouragement to the dogs. Then, remembering something Craig had said about Lindsay's techniques, she took a deep breath. "This land is your land, this land is my land . . ." she sang. The dogs barked and put on a little more speed.

Nancy lost all sense of time. All that mattered was getting George safely home. So far the sled was staying upright, and the dogs were running as though they knew the way.

The snow continued to fall, leaving a thick blanket of white on top of George. Nancy smiled. Snow was a good insulator. It would help keep George warm.

She was singing another rousing chorus of "This Land Is Your Land" to the dogs, when she heard dogs barking behind her. Steve and his team were rapidly catching up. Nancy turned to wave.

Her headlight cast a beacon far enough so that she could see beyond the dogs to the musher who stood on the runners. His suit was light blue, and a lock of blond hair had escaped from his knit cap.

Craig!

He must have been faking unconsciousness back at the cabin, Nancy realized. Somehow he had overpowered Steve and taken the dogs from him. Her heart began to pound. "Oh, hurry!" she called to the dogs, forgetting the commands she had learned.

"Give it up, Nancy!" Craig cried out. "You can't beat me on a dogsled."

Nancy gave the sled a forward push, trying to get the dogs to run faster.

Craig was getting closer.

Fighting for her life and George's, racing through an Alaskan snowstorm, Nancy started singing again. As if to show her approval, Butterscotch turned and barked at Nancy. The dogs picked up speed.

"It won't work!" Craig yelled.

Nancy sang louder. He hates this song, she remembered. Maybe because it works!

The trail was too narrow for Craig to pass her. She tried to remember how much farther it was before the trail widened again.

They were still in the forest when Nancy saw the trees begin to thin out. In just a few yards the trail would be wide enough so that Craig could pull up alongside her.

As soon as he saw the broadening of the trail, Craig shouted to his dogs, quickening their pace. An instant later he had pulled his sled even with Nancy's.

"End of the line," he said with an evil grin.

Nancy shouted to Butterscotch. The lead dog barked her command to the rest of the team, but the dogs could go no faster.

From the corner of her eye, Nancy saw a movement on Craig's sled. What was he up to? she wondered fearfully.

Craig reached into the basket and pulled out a coiled whip.

Nancy bit her lip. "Easy, Butterscotch," she called, hoping her voice sounded more reassuring than she felt. "It'll be all right."

Nancy started singing again. It was all she could do. She knew how Lindsay's dogs hated the sound of a whip. She'd seen firsthand how they reacted to loud noises. Nancy was not a skilled racer who could control a team that ran wild. All she could do was try to prevent them from spooking.

Craig lifted the whip over his head.

Nancy raised her voice in song.

Crack! The sound of the whip echoed through the night.

Butterscotch held fast for a second when the other dogs started to tug on the line. Nancy felt the sled gain momentum as terror propelled the dogs to get as far from the frightening noise as they could.

The team swerved, and for a second Nancy felt the sled begin to slip. Then Butterscotch barked a short command. Though the other dogs yipped their disapproval, they obeyed. The sled continued to gain speed.

Nancy gripped the handlebar tightly and looked to her right. Craig was still there. He gazed at her and touched a mocking hand to his cap.

In that instant, a snowshoe hare hopped across the trail. Craig's dogs swerved to the right to chase the rabbit. When he realized what was happening, Craig quickly tugged on the handlebar.

But it was too late. With a sickening thud, the sled flipped over and slammed against a tree.

There was a blur of blue as Craig let go of the handlebar. Then a small avalanche of snow came down from the tree and buried his still form in a deep drift.

Chapter

Sixteen

Nancy gasped and turned her eyes away. For a moment she thought of stopping, but then she realized there was nothing she could do to help Craig out here.

"Home, Butterscotch, home!" Nancy cried. Quickly the sled pulled out of the forest. The wind was stronger, blowing snow into Nancy's face. Despite her heavy clothes and face mask, her fingers were numb and her face ached. The ride went on and on, like a nightmare.

At last the trail became familiar, and the dogs ran more quickly, knowing they were close to home.

At the sound of her dogs' barking, Lindsay ran from the barn. "You're safe!"

"Help George!" Nancy shouted as she pulled the dog team to a stop. With Lindsay's help, she tugged her woozy friend out from under her warm blanket of snow and wool. Quickly they bundled her into the car.

"We'd better call the police," Nancy said as they drove to the Wilcox house.

"I already did," Lindsay told her. "I wasn't sure where the cabin was, so I called Amanda. She gave the police directions."

Minutes later Nancy and Lindsay supported George as they brought her into the Wilcox house. Carson and Henry ran toward the girls, a babble of questions tumbling from their lips.

Nancy held up one hand. "Wait just a minute, please," she said with a tired laugh. She and Lindsay helped George into the den and deposited her on the couch. Then Nancy flopped down beside her.

"Okay, *now* I'm ready to talk. . . ."

"Are you sure you're okay?" Henry Wilcox asked George for at least the sixth time.

George nodded. By the time the doctor had arrived, she was already recovering from the effects of the sedative. His announcement that there was no permanent damage only confirmed what she'd been telling everyone—that she'd be fine.

The doorbell rang, and Henry jumped to his

feet. He was hoping, Nancy knew, that it was the police returning with Steve and Craig.

Nancy watched his face fall as Amanda came into the den.

"I wanted to make sure . . . everyone was okay," Amanda said in response to Nancy's unspoken question. Something in Amanda's voice told Nancy her concern was for Steve.

"I didn't expect you," Henry told Amanda. He started to say something more, then swallowed his words.

"You mean because your son and I aren't dating anymore?" Amanda asked.

Henry nodded.

"I guess I'm more involved in this than you know," Amanda said. She looked at Nancy.

Nancy flashed her a warm smile. It couldn't have been easy for her to come to the Wilcox house, but here she was.

"Amanda gave me the last clues," Nancy told her father and Henry. "It's because of her telling me about the cabin that I was able to find George."

Amanda's smile was bittersweet. "At least one good thing came out of losing my ring."

"Your ring? What happened?" Lindsay looked at her friend's hand and exclaimed, "You loved that ring!"

It was Amanda's turn to explain, and she made no attempt to excuse herself for her mistakes. "I guess I was lucky that Mr. Feder was willing to buy the ring," she said.

Henry slipped quietly out of the room.

"There's still one thing I don't know," Lindsay said with a long look at George. "Why did Craig kidnap you in the first place?"

"I guess you could say I was in the wrong place at the wrong time," George told her. "I woke up early, but Nancy had already gone into Anchorage, so I decided to go out to the barn. I found Craig there, loading ivory figurines into the bags of dog food."

"He knew George would tell me about it," Nancy continued, "so they struggled and he knocked her out. Then he put her on the sled, disguised as cargo."

George looked at her wristwatch. "Where are they?" she asked in a worried voice.

"Steve will be okay," Nancy answered with more confidence than she felt. By now the police should have found both Craig and Steve.

"What if the fire goes out in that cabin?" Amanda asked. "It's so cold outside. If the fire goes out, Steve could . . ." Henry walked back into the room, and she broke off.

"You don't have to mince words with me, Amanda," Henry told her. "I'm well aware of the dangers of an Alaskan snowstorm. But I also know my son. He's a winner."

147

Henry spoke with such pride that everyone in the room smiled. Nancy wished she had a tape recording. Better yet, she wished Steve were there to hear his father praise him.

Henry smiled at Amanda. "I suggest you visit Mr. Feder tomorrow. I'm going to arrange for him to sell me your ring." A look of wonder crossed Amanda's face as Henry continued, "You and I can work out the terms of repayment."

Amanda's smile said more than her words could. "Thank you," she cried, hugging Henry Wilcox until he flushed with embarrassment.

Carson rose and tossed another log onto the fire. As he did, they heard the sound of someone leaning on the doorbell. Then the front door opened.

"Anyone home?" Steve yelled.

Within moments the den was empty, as everyone ran into the hallway. Steve and two police officers stood inside the front door, stomping the snow off their boots.

"You're safe!" Henry clasped his son to him, then held him at arm's length and studied him.

Steve sighed happily. "It feels great to be back, I can tell you that." When he saw Amanda, the smile on his face told Nancy he was ready to put their past problems behind them. Then his eyes moved to George. "Are you okay?"

"Yes, thanks to you," George replied. "Nancy told me everything that happened, and I know I might not be standing here now if it weren't for you."

Nancy couldn't hold her questions back any longer. "Steve, what happened back at the cabin?" she asked. "How did Craig get free? When I saw him, I was afraid . . ."

"You don't need to say it." For a moment Steve's face looked haggard. "It was pretty scary.

"I guess Craig was only momentarily stunned after I tripped him," Steve went on. "I don't know how he got free of those ropes, but just as I finished harnessing the dogs, he came after me. We struggled, and he knocked me out—for real this time. He left me lying in the snow and locked the cabin door—I guess he figured I'd die of exposure. Lucky for me, when I came to I was able to jimmy open a window and get back inside. After that all I could do was wait for someone to find me. Boy, was I glad when these guys turned up on their snowmobiles!" He grinned at the two police officers.

"We got a little lost in the forest," one of the officers put in, "but we got there eventually."

"How'd you get the dogs back?" Amanda wanted to know.

"I drove the team," Steve said modestly.

"After all you went through, you were still able to mush?" Amanda gave him an admiring look.

"Didn't I tell you my son's a winner?" Henry demanded jovially.

A grin of pure pleasure crossed Steve's face as he led the way back into the den.

"Did you find Craig?" Carson Drew asked one of the police officers.

"Sure did. Steve spotted him lying beside the trail. Miller's in custody, and he's already started talking. He told us about his accomplice in Seattle and about how he distributed the ivory here in Anchorage."

The other officer nodded. "By tomorrow night we'll have this smuggling ring disbanded."

Carson turned to Nancy. "It looks like this case is closed."

"Nancy, I don't know how to thank you," Henry told her.

Nancy shook her head. "There's no need. I was glad to help."

After the police left, Carson and Henry went to the study. Steve turned to the four girls. "I want you all to be my witnesses, because what I have to say is very painful."

He paused. Then he turned to Lindsay and grinned. "You were right. Your dogs are better than mine."

Lindsay raised one eyebrow. "What makes you say that?"

"Look at how well an amateur like Nancy did driving them," he responded. But the teasing look he gave Nancy told her he didn't mean the comment maliciously.

George put both hands on her hips and glared at Steve. "Did it ever occur to you that Nancy might be a natural dogsledder?" she demanded loyally. "It could be Nancy's skill, not the dogs, that got us back here."

Steve looked thoughtful. "You might be right," he admitted. As Nancy watched, a speculative expression crossed his face. Turning to her, he asked, "Would you like to race my dogs in the Solstice Derby?"

Nancy pretended to consider Steve's offer. Then she grinned. "No thanks, Steve. I've already had the ride of a lifetime!"

Nancy's next case:

Ned invites Nancy, Bess, and George to Emerson College's Winter Carnival for four days of nonstop skiing, skating, and sleigh riding. But a jewel heist on campus puts a big chill on the weekend, and the police believe they have their man cold. His name is Rob Harper, and he's one of Ned's best friends!

Convinced of Rob's innocence, Nancy undertakes an investigation of her own. But the action on ice proves more slippery than she expected. Someone at Emerson is out to teach Nancy a lesson and show her just how dangerous winter sports can be. When it comes to jewelry, some like it hot—and the carnival of crime is heating up fast . . . in *COLD AS ICE,* Case #54 in The Nancy Drew Files™.

Dear Friend,

Heard the latest? It seems just about everyone's talking about the sensational new series set in my hometown. It's called River Heights, and if you haven't heard, you don't know what you're missing!

You know I love to ask questions, so let me ask you a few. Do you like romance? A juicy secret? Do you believe there's life after homework? If so, take it from me, you'll love this exciting series starring the students of River Heights High.

I'd like you to meet Nikki Masters, all-American sweetheart of River Heights High, and Niles Butler, the gorgeous British hunk who makes Nikki's knees shake. And Brittany Tate, leader of the "in" crowd, who knows what she wants and will do just about anything to get it. She's got her eye on supersnob Chip Worthington. Samantha Daley, meanwhile, has fallen for Kyle Kirkwood. He's a social zero, but she's come up with a foolproof plan to turn him into the hottest ticket in town.

It's a thrill-filled world of teen dreams and teen schemes. It's all delicious fun, and it's all waiting for you—in River Heights!

Sincerely,
Nancy Drew

P.S. Turn the page for your own private preview of River Heights #9: *Lies and Whispers*.

Talk of the Town!

Brittany Tate, as devious as she is gorgeous, is out to snare the number-one country-club snob, Chip Worthington. He'd make the perfect boyfriend, her ticket to the top of the River Heights social scene. So what if she can hardly stand the guy?

Lacey Dupree can't forgive herself for the argument she had with boyfriend Rick Stratton just before his near-fatal rock climbing accident. Now that he's finally regained consciousness, the question that weighs most on her heart is, Will he ever forgive her?

Karen Jacobs has never loved any guy the way she loves Ben Newhouse. But the feeling can drive her to the depths of despair. Has Ben *really* gotten over his ex-girlfriend, model Emily Van Patten? And if not, how can Karen ever compete with someone so beautiful?

Ellen Ming is in trouble. Her father's been accused of embezzlement, and now Kim Bishop has accused Ellen of stealing junior class funds! Ellen's only hope is Nancy Drew. Will Nancy find a way to put a stop to the vicious gossip?

THE RUMORS ARE FLYING
IN RIVER HEIGHTS—
CATCH THEM IN
LIES AND WHISPERS!

"Hurry, Ben!" Lacey Dupree urged. "Can't you go any faster?"

"I'm doing the speed limit, Lacey," Ben Newhouse responded.

Lacey impatiently brushed back her halo of long red-gold waves and trained her eyes on the road ahead. Just one more block and they'd be at the hospital. One more block and she could see Rick Stratton, her boyfriend. Rick had finally regained consciousness after a rock-climbing accident.

Ben made a left turn into the hospital parking lot. Lacey opened her door as the car coasted to a stop.

"Whoa, Lacey!" Ben hit the brakes and turned to her. "I know you're anxious, but take it easy, okay?"

"I'm sorry, Ben," Lacey said as she opened the door wider. "I just can't wait. I have to see Rick!"

She slid out of the car and headed for the entrance. Across the lobby she skidded to a stop in front of the bank of elevators.

Jabbing the Up button impatiently, Lacey paused to

take a deep breath. Now that she was actually there, she started to worry again. What would Rick say when he saw her? He might hate her and blame her. If they hadn't had that terrible argument, he wouldn't have fallen during his rock-climbing expedition. He wouldn't have been lying unconscious in the hospital for more than two weeks!

The elevator doors slid open, and Lacey sprang on. She tapped her foot the whole time the elevator rose. As soon as the doors parted, she stepped out.

She thought of how she'd come there, day after day, her heart breaking at the sight of Rick lying unconscious. The pain of it had been hard to bear. But how would it compare to the pain of Rick's rejecting her now?

Rick's door was open. Lacey peeked in. Rick was pale, and there were dark circles under his eyes. His muscular body seemed thin now. He looked ill, Lacey thought, but he'd never looked so good to her.

He glanced up just then. "Lacey," he said.

"Hello, Rick." Lacey couldn't seem to move from the doorway. Did he want her to go to him? She didn't know what to do!

"Oh, Rick," Lacey whispered, her eyes blurring with tears. "I'm so glad you're back."

Couples! Everywhere Brittany Tate looked, she saw nothing but couples. When she got off the school bus, she almost crashed into Mark Giordano and Chris Martinez, king and queen of the jocks. Nikki Masters, the golden girl, was just pulling into a parking space with that adorable Niles Butler. From across the quad, Robin Fisher waved to Nikki and Niles with her boyfriend, Calvin Roth.

Brittany pressed her lips together as she headed up the walk. Robin had really spoiled things for her at the Winter Carnival Ball. She'd let Brittany have it for setting up a fight between Lacey Dupree and Rick Stratton. Robin had actually blamed Brittany for Rick's accident! It was bad enough that Brittany herself had felt guilty for her part in the couple's fight. She didn't need Robin to rub it in. And she certainly didn't need Tim Cooper to hear about it!

He'd been standing in the shadows, listening to every word. The rest of the night had been a disaster. Tim had been icily polite, but it was obvious he wished he was a million miles away. And he'd dumped Brittany on her doorstep like a load of old laundry.

She had come so close to having Tim for a boyfriend. She'd turned over a new leaf and been incredibly nice, and Tim had finally responded. But now Tim thought she was a double-dealing snake.

Brittany would never forgive Robin Fisher. Never. She gave Robin her trademark drop-dead look as she walked by. Robin merely grinned back at her. Brittany tossed her gleaming dark hair and hurried over to Kim Bishop and Samantha Daley, her best friends.

"What's going on with you and Robin?" Kim asked. "I saw that look you gave her."

Brittany shrugged. "That girl should get a life. She didn't like the fact that I went to the ball with her best friend's ex-boyfriend."

Samantha Daley leaned closer, her cinnamon eyes sparkling. "What *did* happen with you and Tim?" she asked in her soft southern drawl.

Kim and Samantha were staring expectantly. Brittany thought fast. She leaned over and said in a whisper, "I'll tell you a secret. That hunk Tim Cooper is just the teeniest bit boring. Nikki can have him." Brittany shook back her thick, dark hair and laughed. "I'm looking for someone a little wilder."

Normally, that comment would impress Samantha and Kim. They'd demand more details, wondering what she was planning. But Samantha and Kim were barely listening to her. They were staring over her head.

"Here come the guys," Kim said.

Brittany turned around. Jeremy Pratt and Kyle Kirkwood, Kim and Samantha's boyfriends, were heading for them. Kyle's face brightened at the sight of Samantha. Brittany wanted to throw up.

"Hello, gorgeous," Jeremy said to Kim. She smiled regally. The two of them were such a pain, Brittany thought impatiently. They thought they were the hottest thing to hit River Heights High since Mexican Day in the cafeteria.

"We were just talking about the country club dance this weekend," Jeremy said. "It's going to be major."

"It sounds okay," Kyle said. "I'm not a big fan of the country club, but Samantha really wants to go."

"I can't wait," Samantha said. She slipped her hand into Kyle's.

Brittany tuned them out. She was glad to be reminded of the country club dance. It would be the first big function she would attend as a member. It was time, Brittany decided, for her to be back on top. That meant snaring a fantastic new boyfriend.

"Who's going?" she asked Jeremy.

"Oh, the usual country club crowd," Jeremy said, waving a hand. "No one you'd know."

Brittany's hand tightened on her books. Jeremy

was so slimy he must have crawled out of a swamp. He never let her forget that she had only recently become a member—and only a junior member at that.

"Some of the college crowd will probably be there," Kim added.

Brittany sighed. "I'm sick of the college crowd," she said. "Jack Reilly called the other night, but I refused to speak to him. Who else is going, Kim?"

"The snobs from Talbot and Fox Hill, of course," Kim replied. Talbot and Fox Hill were the boys' and girls' private schools in River Heights.

"I just hope Chip Worthington isn't there," Jeremy muttered.

Brittany stifled a grin. Kim had told her that Chip had nearly rearranged the aristocratic Pratt profile a while ago. She could understand why Jeremy wouldn't want to see him again.

"You could always hire a bodyguard, Jeremy," Brittany said sweetly.

"It's not that I'm afraid of him," Jeremy returned quickly. "He makes all these comments about Kim, just to give me grief. He keeps leering at her and saying things like, 'What are you doing with the most beautiful girl in River Heights, Pratt?' Stuff like that. It's totally annoying."

"Really," Kim agreed, tossing her shiny blond hair.

Jeremy might hate it, but Kim wasn't too upset, Brittany was sure. Who wouldn't like being called the most beautiful girl in River Heights? Of course, Chip Worthington hadn't met Brittany Tate yet.

Then it hit her. Why not go after Chip? Brittany was bored with all the boys at school. Why not stake out some new territory? Let Kim and Jeremy be king and queen of River Heights High. Brittany and Chip would run the town!

Ellen Ming walked to the student council meeting. She took her usual seat and waited for Ms. Rose, the student council faculty advisor, to show up.

While she waited, Ellen began to feel uneasy. She saw Juliann Wade, the treasurer of the student council, whisper something to Patty Casey, who was the secretary. They both glanced at Ellen, then quickly looked away.

Ben Newhouse arrived, and then Kevin Hoffman came in. Kevin grinned warmly at Ellen as he slid into his seat.

Feeling a blush start on her cheeks, Ellen stared down at the tabletop. Sometimes the feelings she'd had when she had her crush on Kevin came back. Nothing had ever come of her silly crush, not even one date. Ellen knew she was too serious for Kevin, who was full of jokes and mischief. There was something about his unruly red-brown hair and easy grin that made her smile.

Ms. Rose walked into the room with her brisk step. "Good afternoon, people. Let's get started," she said. "Today the first item on the agenda is the proposal for a luau. A committee has already been formed, headed by Ellen Ming. Since the committee will be mainly using the decorations from the tropical theme that we scrapped for the Winter Carnival, the cost won't be too high. And the committee has high hopes that the record and tape sales will take care of the rest of the costs. Ellen, how's the whole plan going?"

"Fine," Ellen said. "We have volunteers lined up to handle the record and tape sales."

"Sounds great. Keep us posted," Ms. Rose said. She studied her notes again. "Now, if there's nothing else on the luau, let's get to—"

"Ms. Rose?" Juliann Wade waved her hand in the air.

Ms. Rose looked up. "Yes, Juliann?"

"I was wondering who's handling the proceeds from the record sale."

Ms. Rose frowned at Juliann, but she turned to Ellen. "Ellen?"

Ellen saw Patty Casey poke Juliann underneath the table. Ellen's heart began to flutter. "I am," she said in a shaky voice.

"What's your point, Juliann?" Ms. Rose asked frostily. Ellen had a feeling Ms. Rose knew what the girl was getting at—and she didn't like it.

Juliann shook back her blond hair defiantly. "I'm just wondering if we should reconsider having Ellen handle the funds, that's all. I'd be glad to take over."

"I agree with Juliann," Patty said quickly.

Ms. Rose studied the two girls. "And what exactly do you agree with, Patty?"

Patty's eyes traveled around the room as if she was seeking an answer. "Well, that maybe Juliann should take charge of the funds. She *is* school treasurer."

Juliann nodded. "Especially under the circumstances . . ." she said meaningfully, letting her voice trail off.

The room was quiet. Did that mean that people were shocked or that they agreed with Juliann? Ellen felt sick. How could this be happening? They thought she wasn't trustworthy enough to take charge of the money!

She felt Ben stir next to her, but before he could say anything, Kevin Hoffman spoke up.

"That's very nice of you, Juliann." Kevin's voice was calm, but it held a deadly undertone Ellen had never heard before. "Ellen *has* been doing two jobs since Lacey Dupree has dropped out temporarily. She could feel overloaded. I'm sure those were the circumstances you were talking about, right?"

Juliann swallowed. She glanced at Ms. Rose, who was giving her a cold stare. "Of course," she mumbled.

"But Ellen is doing such a fantastic job," Kevin went on steadily, "as usual, that as long as she feels she can handle it, I see no reason to make a change. Do you feel you can handle this on top of Lacey's responsibilities, Ellen?"

Ellen looked at Kevin. His green eyes had a fierce look. He nodded at her, giving her courage. He was on her side! "Yes," she managed to choke out.

"Then let's not waste any more time," Ms. Rose stated crisply. "We have more important business."

Everyone in the room relaxed, except for Ellen. Her heart was racing. Kevin had saved her neck, all right, but she couldn't get over the fact that Juliann had been so cruel in the first place.

Suddenly Ellen realized that she hadn't thought of the worst thing about her father's being accused of embezzlement. He might not go to jail, but his life still could be destroyed. He would always be under a cloud of suspicion.

Ellen had just seen something she wished she hadn't. People could take a rumor or a suspicion and they could use it to disgrace someone. If Ellen was facing that kind of attitude in a student council meeting, what would Mr. Ming face at work? Ellen shivered with foreboding. Things could get a lot worse before they got better.

Brittany scanned the crowd at the country club dance.

"Who are you looking for?" Samantha asked.

"I'm just shopping, Samantha dear," Brittany said distractedly. But just as she finished speaking, she caught sight of Chip Worthington. He was tall and seemed assured, as if he owned the country club. He scanned the room with a bored air.

Brittany willed him to turn around and look at her, but he turned his attention to his friends. She sighed. She'd have to get Kim to introduce her.

Brittany saw her chance. Kim and Jeremy were standing on the sidelines, having a soda. Brittany watched as Chip joined them. Jeremy's face darkened in a scowl, but Chip was grinning as he talked. He was probably tormenting Jeremy, Brittany thought. Maybe Chip wasn't so bad, after all.

Quickly Brittany walked across the room to Kim and Jeremy.

"Hi," she interrupted breathlessly. "I haven't had a chance to talk to you guys all night." She fixed her dark eyes on Chip. "Oh, I'm sorry, am I interrupting?"

"Not at all," Chip said. His clear green eyes flicked over her, and he gave a lazy grin. "Not at all," he repeated. "Who are *you,* and why haven't I met you yet?"

Brittany smiled back. "How about meeting me right now?" she said. "I'm Brittany Tate."

"Chip Worthington," Chip answered.

Kim stirred beside Brittany. She might not be able to stand Chip, but it was clear she didn't like Brittany stealing his attention, either. "Brittany became a junior member of the club recently," she said. "That's probably why you don't know her."

"I suppose you go to school with Pratt, here," Chip said. He casually ran a hand through his straight, side-parted brown hair.

"That's right. Do you go to Talbot?"

"Of course," Chip replied. "If every Worthington didn't enroll, the school would collapse and sink right into the ground. We practically built the place back in the Stone Age. Now we just throw pots of money at it to keep it running."

Brittany laughed her silvery laugh. What a snob! she thought. Kim was right, for once. "Well, thank heavens you enrolled, then," she said. "We wouldn't want anything to happen to Talbot."

"For sure," Chip agreed lazily. "And what do you do at River Heights High, Brittany?"

"Well, I'm on the school paper, the *Record,*" Brittany said. "I have my own column, called 'Off the Record.'"

"Nice name," Chip said.

Why did every remark he made sound as though he was making fun of her? Brittany wondered. But his eyes were definitely expressing approval. Did he like her or not?

Nikki Masters parked her car and followed Ellen Ming into the coffee shop. After they ordered sodas, Nikki looked at her expectantly.

"What's on your mind, Ellen?" Nikki leaned forward, her hands cupping her glass. Her blue eyes were kind and patient.

Ellen suddenly felt afraid. Nikki Masters had been in trouble once—that was true. But she was well past it now. She was beautiful and popular, and nice, too. Would she be able to sympathize with Ellen's problem?

"Ellen, if it makes it any easier for you, I know what it's like to need help," Nikki said softly. "I know it's hard to ask. But believe me, it's better. I want to do what I can."

Ellen's fears dissolved under the balm of Nikki's soft words. She gripped her glass and poured out her story, barely pausing for breath.

"I've gone over the junior class bank account more times than you can imagine," Ellen concluded. "I discovered right away that two deposits I recorded in the ledger didn't match the bank's record of deposits."

"How do you make the deposits?" Nikki asked. "At the bank?"

"No, it closes at three, so I use the night deposit slot," Ellen told her. "The two deposits were from last Friday and this Monday—from the record and tape sale. Each day I totalled the receipts, filled out a deposit slip, and sealed the envelope. Then I locked it in a drawer in the student council office. After school, I took it to the bank."

Nikki nodded thoughtfully. "So somebody got to the money while it was in the drawer. The person took out the bills and resealed the envelope.

"That's what I figure," Ellen said. "But, Nikki, who's going to believe that it wasn't me? After what's happened with my father, I mean."

"I believe it wasn't you," Nikki assured her. "Others will, too. Not everybody is like Kim Bishop, Ellen."

"But I'm class treasurer, Nikki. If my name isn't cleared, I'll lose the office."

"I have an idea," Nikki said slowly. "Would you mind if one more person knew the story? Not someone from school," she added hastily.

"Who?" Ellen asked, puzzled.

"Nancy Drew. She's a good friend of mine, and she lives next door."

"Wow," Ellen breathed. "Do you think it would be okay?"

"We won't know until I call her," Nikki said briskly. She reached into the pocket of her jeans for some change. "Can I?"

"Right now?" Ellen gulped. "I guess so. After all, how can I turn down a world-famous detective?"

Want more? Get the whole story in River Heights #9, *Lies and Whispers*.